For half a minute or so it rocked and swayed
against the sky-line.

HIGHWAY PIRATES

OR, THE SECRET PLACE AT COVERTHORNE

By

HAROLD AVERY

HIGHWAY PIRATES.

CHAPTER I.

A DAY OF TROUBLE.

"They've seen us! Run for it!"

My chosen friend, Miles Coverthorne, was the speaker. He sprang to his feet as he uttered the words, and darted like a rabbit into the bushes, I myself following hard at his heels. The seasons seem to have come earlier in those days, and though May was not out, the woods and countryside appeared clothed with all the richness of leafy June.

At headlong speed we dashed through the underwood, stung by hazel switches which struck us across the face like whips, and staggering as our feet caught in thick tufts of grass.

"Who is it—keepers?" I inquired.

"No; 'Eagles'!" was the quick reply.

If anything had been needed to quicken my pace, this last word would have served the purpose. We both rushed wildly onward, as though our very lives were at stake.

It may be guessed that Miles did not mean to imply that a number of real eagles were swooping down upon us with the intention of bearing us away to some rocky crags, there to form an appetizing repast for their young; the word had, in this case, a special meaning, to explain which a slight digression will be necessary.

Many things have altered since the year 1830, and in no direction are greater changes manifested than in the schools and school life of that period compared with those of the present day. What the modern boy at Hobworth's School (so called after its worthy founder) would think of the place if suddenly transferred back to the days when I went there as a boarder, I cannot imagine. Whole chapters might be devoted to a comparison of the past with the present, but for the purposes of our story only one point need be considered, and that is the great difference in the style and character of recreation out of school hours.

Though organized games, such as cricket, no doubt existed in the big public schools, they were unknown at Hobworth's. Such sports as prisoner's base, marbles, and an elaborate form of leap-frog called—if I remember rightly—"fly-the-garter," we certainly indulged in; but, as might be expected, such amusements did not always satisfy the bolder spirits—the result being that these found vent for their adventurous inclinations in various expeditions, which more than once landed them in serious trouble with farmers and gamekeepers.

I cannot say that there was any vicious intention in these raids and forays. It was perhaps difficult for us boys to see the justice of certain men claiming all the birds' eggs, squirrels, or hazel-nuts in the neighbourhood, especially as these things were of no value to their avowed owners. Again, if pheasants were disturbed, or fences broken, or perhaps a rabbit knocked over for the joy of subsequently cooking it surreptitiously in a coffee-pot, it was, after all, a very small matter, and not worth making a fuss about. So, at least, the youngster of that period would have argued.

Those were not happy times for the small and weak. Brute force was far too highly esteemed, and the champion fighter of a school was thought as much or even more of than the leading cricket or football player is to-day. It was an unpardonable sin for a small boy to sneak, but the cruelty and oppression of the more evil-minded of his elders was hardly deemed worthy of censure. Out of school hours very little notice was taken by masters of how their pupils employed their time, and as long as the latter refrained from bringing the place about their ears with any acts of particularly flagrant mischief, they were left pretty much to their own devices.

Partly for mutual protection against the violence of their fellows, and partly in pursuit of the questionable forms of recreation already referred to, the boys had formed themselves into a number of "tribes," each under the leadership of some heavy-fisted chieftain to whom they swore allegiance, at the same time sharing all their worldly possessions with the other members of the band.

In course of time these various small communities became gradually absorbed into two large rival bands known as the "Foxes" and the "Eagles," the peculiarity of name being due to an exciting story of adventure among the Indians which had been going the round of the school; for books of that kind were, in those days, a rare and highly-prized possession.

Skirmishes between parties of the two tribes were of frequent occurrence, and expeditions with various objects, and not unfrequently exciting endings, were indulged in almost every half-holiday afternoon. Miles and myself were numbered among the "Foxes," while at the head of the "Eagles" was a notorious bully named Ben Liddle, who possessed all the nature and none of the nobility of the actual savage. This leader had lately laid claim to all the woods and country on the north side of the road which passed the school, as the hunting-ground of the "Eagles," and had thrown out dark hints of a terrible vengeance which should be meted out to any luckless "Fox" who should be captured encroaching on this preserve.

As this meant nothing less than calmly appropriating all the places where any good sport could be obtained, the claim was naturally resented by the "Foxes;" and though Kerry, our chief, had not as yet made any public pronouncement on the subject, it was understood that before long the matter would be discussed, probably in a grand pitched battle between the tribes, when this and other causes of disagreement would be settled once for all.

But even Ben Liddle's threats were not sufficient to keep enterprising "Foxes" on the south side of the road. Miles and I had already made several expeditions into the forbidden territory, perhaps rather enjoying the extra risk of capture by "Eagles," added to the chance of being chased by keepers. On this particular Saturday afternoon we had penetrated into the depths of a favourite haunt named Patchley Wood. The arms of an "Indian" at such times, I might explain, were a big catapult, a pocketful of pebbles, and a short stick with a lump of lead at the end, in shape somewhat resembling a life-preserver. This weapon—known to us as a "squaler"—was capable of being flung with great force and precision. With the whole of this outfit we were duly provided.

We had been in the woods perhaps half an hour, and had lain down to rest at the foot of a tree, when my companion's quick eye detected the approach of the enemy, with the result that we immediately took flight in the manner which has already been described.

At headlong speed we dashed off through the bushes, regardless of the noise we made; for any hope we might hitherto have entertained of escaping unobserved had been dispelled by the shout sent up by the "Eagles" the moment we moved. On we ran, the enemy following hard in pursuit, crashing through the underwood, while Liddle's voice rang out yelling directions to his followers, heedless of the risk he ran of attracting the notice of the keepers. If captured by the rival chief, we knew we might expect no mercy; and though the pair of us were pretty swift-footed, we felt that nothing short of a stroke of luck would save us, for among the "braves" now in pursuit were some of the best runners in the school.

To lessen still more our hope of escape, before us rose a gentle slope, on which the underwood grew so sparse and thin as to render it certain that we should be seen by our pursuers as we breasted the rise. We laboured on up the hill, gasping for breath as we neared the top; then a yell of triumph from behind, as our pursuers caught sight of us, goaded us to pull ourselves together in one last effort to escape.

Plunging into the thickets, which now became again more dense, we had not gone twenty yards when Miles caught his foot in a root, and came down headlong. He recovered himself immediately from the shock of the fall, and attempted to scramble to his feet, but sank down again with a smothered cry of pain.

"I'm done for," he said. "I've twisted my ankle. Go on; don't wait!"

Anxious as I was to outdistance the "Eagles," I had certainly no thought of leaving Miles to their tender mercies, and glancing round I saw, close at hand, the trunk of a large tree which had recently been felled, together with a large heap of branches which had been lopped off by the woodcutters. Though a very poor one, it was our only chance; so, half carrying Miles, I got him to the spot. We flung ourselves down in a little vacant space between the trunk and the pile of wood, and at the same moment heard Liddle and the foremost of his band gain the summit of the slope, and come bursting through the bushes.

Possibly if we had had a better start, the "Eagles" might have searched for and found us; as it was, they never thought we should pull up with them so close at our heels, and the wood pile was such a poor place of concealment that it did not seem to attract their attention or arouse their suspicion. They rushed on, whooping as they went; and those following behind, no doubt thinking that their comrades in front had us in view, paid no heed to anything but the headlong chase. Thus it came about that, much to our surprise, as we lay panting on the ground we had the satisfaction of hearing the last of our pursuers go racing past, leaving us unmolested to recover our wind and make off in another direction.

"I thought my ankle was broken," muttered Miles, "but it's only a sharp twist. I think I can hobble along; and we'd better get out of this as soon as we can, for they may find they've overrun us, and turn back."

We paused for a moment to get our bearings.

"The road must be close here," I remarked. "Once across it we shall be in our own territory, and can easily escape."

Taking the lead, and with my companion hobbling along in the rear, I headed for the edge of the wood. Fortune seemed to be favouring us, for we found a gap in the hedge through which Miles was able to scramble in spite of his disabled foot. I followed with a jump, and we were just congratulating ourselves on having outwitted the hostile "tribe," when a long-drawn yell, which we at once recognized as their war-cry, caused us to turn our heads. Away down the road stood a solitary "brave," who had evidently been sent there by Liddle to give warning if we should break out of the wood. The yell was immediately answered by others, and a moment later several of our foes came bursting through the hedge, though at a spot some distance beyond the post occupied by their scout.

Escape seemed out of the question. It was impossible for Miles, with his wrenched ankle, to scramble over ditches and hedges, and we had no choice but to keep on the road. In despair we turned and ran towards the school, Coverthorne hobbling and hopping along as best he could, with clenched teeth and subdued groans. Then suddenly, as we turned a corner, we came face to face with a gentleman on horseback, who on seeing us abruptly reined in his steed.

My first fearful thought was that this must be Squire Eastman, the owner of the woods in which we had been trespassing; but a second glance showed me that I was mistaken, and at the same time I heard Miles exclaim,–

"Hullo, young man!" remarked the horseman; "you seem in a hurry. What's the matter? Late for school?"

"No, thank you, uncle," gasped the boy; "it's only—only a game."

Mr. Nicholas Coverthorne was a hard-featured man, with cold gray eyes and a rather harsh voice. He rode a big black horse, and seemed to control the animal with a wrist of iron. Something in his manner and appearance caused me to take an instinctive dislike to him, though at the time of this our first meeting I certainly had reason to feel grateful for his opportune appearance, which was undoubtedly the means of delivering us out of the hands of our enemies. As the leading "braves" turned the corner, they promptly wheeled about and fled back the way they had come, shouting out to their comrades that we had been caught by the squire, at which intelligence the band quickly dispersed over the fields, and made their way back to the school by different routes.

A few more sentences passed between uncle and nephew, and though not any more observant of such things than most boys, it struck me at once that the relationship between them did not appear to be very cordial. Mr. Coverthorne explained that he had been over to see a neighbouring farmer about the sale of a horse.

"I'm going to stay with a friend at Round Green to-night," he said. "It's rather too far to get here from home and back in the same day, though I daresay Nimrod would take me all the way if I let him."

The speaker laughed in a mirthless manner, and after a few more questions as to how his nephew was getting on at school, and when the holidays began, wished us good-bye, and, with a parting nod, went on his way.

Miles seemed glad to get the interview ended, and turned to me with what seemed almost a sigh of relief as the horseman disappeared round the bend in the road.

"Come on," he said. "The 'Eagles' may be hiding somewhere, and rush out as soon as the horse has passed them. That was my uncle Nicholas," he continued, as he hobbled along. "I don't think I ever told you about him. He's my father's only brother, but they quarrelled some years ago, and now they never meet or speak."

"Why was that?" I asked.

"Oh, it was about the property. My grandfather left Coverthorne and almost all the land to my father, and Uncle Nicholas had only a small farm called Stonebank; but before that he'd had a lot of money to enable him to start in business, and he lost it all in speculation. He said at my grandfather's death that the property and land ought to have been divided, but my father told him he had already had his share in money."

"Your people have lived at Coverthorne an awful time, haven't they?" I asked.

"Oh yes. It's a dear old house, with low rooms and big latticed windows with stone mullions, and a broad oak staircase. There's an old sundial in the garden which was put there in Queen Elizabeth's reign; and what's more, the house has a secret place which nobody can find."

"A secret place! what's that?" I inquired, pricking up my ears.

"Why, it's a little secret chamber or hiding-place which has been made somewhere in the building years and years ago, when there might be chances of people having to be concealed to save their lives. There is a rule in our family, handed down from one generation to another, that the whereabouts of the secret place must only be known to the owner of the house, and be told by him to the heir when he is twenty-one."

"Then you yourself don't know where it is?"

"No; my father will tell me when I come of age. Of course if he were dying, or were going on a long journey from which he might never return, or anything of that kind were to happen, he would tell me at once, else the secret might be lost for ever."

"Is it big enough for a man to get into?"

"Oh yes—big enough for two people to stand in, so father says."

"Then surely it must be easy to find. I can't see how it's possible for there to be a little room in a house without people knowing it is there. I believe I could find it for you if you gave me the chance."

Miles laughed.

"You'd better come over and try," he answered. "Now, that's a good idea. You must come and stay with me for part of the summer holidays, and we'll have heaps of fun. It would be jolly to have you, for I often find it dull with no cousins or friends of my own age."

The proposal struck me as most delightful. During the last few moments I had been picturing up the ancient house, with its old-world associations and romantic hidden chamber, and comparing it, in my mind, with the prosaic red-brick building in which my own parents lived. Moreover, Coverthorne, I knew, was situated on the sea-coast, and only about a quarter of a mile from the summit of the rugged cliffs. I had often listened with envy to my friend's tales of wrecks and smugglers, and longed to have an opportunity of wandering over the wide headlands, climbing the rocks and exploring the caves. Now the prospect of such treats being actually in store made me feel quite a thrill of delightful anticipation.

I had not finished thanking Miles and telling him how much I should like to come, when we reached the school. Passing through a side door we entered the playground, and were almost immediately surrounded by a crowd of "Foxes," who had somehow got wind of our escape from the "Eagles," and were eager to have a detailed account of the adventure.

Telling our story, and receiving the congratulations of the other members of our "tribe," so much occupied our attention that we hardly noticed the sound of a horse galloping down the road and stopping in front of the schoolhouse; but a few moments later Sparrow, the porter, crossed the playground and, addressing Miles, told him he was wanted at once by Dr. Bagley.

A message of that kind from the headmaster usually meant that there was trouble in the wind.

"Hullo!" exclaimed a boy named Seaton, "what's the row, I wonder? He'll want you next, Eden. You must have been seen in the woods, and the squire has sent some one over to complain."

Reluctantly Miles followed the porter. In no very enviable frame of mind I waited, expecting every minute to be ordered to appear before the doctor in his study. Still no such message came, nor did Miles return to inform us of his fate. We heard the horseman ride away again, but the height of the playground wall prevented our seeing whether he really were one of the men-servants from the Hall. A little later Liddle returned with a band of his "braves;" but the "Foxes" being also present in force, he could only shake his fist at me, and repeat his former threats of what he would do if he caught us on the hunting-ground of the "Eagles." At length the bell rang, and we moved towards the house.

Hardly had I entered the door when I met Sparrow.

"Have you heard the news, Master Eden?" he exclaimed. "Dreadful—dreadful! Poor Master Coverthorne! His father's been shot—mortally wounded—and is most probably dead by this time. It's a great question if the young gentleman will ever see him alive."

"What!" I cried—"Mr. Coverthorne shot! How did it happen?"

"It's true enough," answered Sparrow. "I had it all from the messenger himself. Mr. Coverthorne was out shooting with a party, and a gen'leman's gun went off by accident as he was climbing a hedge. Mr. Coverthorne was shot in the breast. They got a trap, and took him to the Crown at

Welmington, and sent for a surgeon. He wanted particular to see his son, so one of the postboys rode over; but it's hardly likely the young gentleman will get there in time."

"What a dreadful thing!" I muttered. "Poor Miles! I wish I could have seen him before he went."

The news of this terrible blow which had so suddenly fallen on my companion shocked me almost as much as if the trouble had been my own. When adventuring together into the woods that afternoon, how little he imagined what the immediate future had in store!

I sat down with the rest in the long, bare dining-room, but had little heart to eat; the thought of Miles being hurried along the country road, not knowing whether he would find his father alive or dead, weighed down my spirits. If his father died, the only relative he would have in the world, besides his widowed mother, would be his uncle Nicholas; and remembering the latter's hard face and harsh voice, and the story of the brothers' quarrel, my mind was filled with dark forebodings for the future of my friend.

CHAPTER II.

THE KNOCKING ON THE WALL.

It was ten days before I saw Miles again; then he returned to school for the last three weeks of the half. Seeing him dressed in black, and noticing the unaccustomed look of sadness on his usually cheerful face, boylike I felt for a moment shy of meeting him; but with the first hearty hand-grip all feeling of restraint vanished, and I was able to give him the assurance of my sympathy and friendship. Then it was that I heard for the first time how he had arrived at Welmington too late to see his father alive—a fact which must have added greatly to the heaviness of the blow and the keenness of his grief.

Naturally, for the time, he had no heart to join in our usual amusements; and his rough, though for the most part good natured, schoolboy comrades showed their sympathy in allowing him to go his own ways. Just then "Foxes" and "Eagles" had buried the hatchet, owing to the fact that a spell of hot weather had set in, and the members of both "tribes" went amicably, nearly every day, to bathe in a neighbouring stream.

The majority of the boarders were thus engaged one afternoon, and Miles and I had the playground to ourselves. We were sitting on a seat under a shady tree, and something perhaps in the restful quiet of the place encouraged my companion to unburden himself and take me into his confidence. I had noticed a troubled look on his face, and inquired whether anything was weighing on his mind.

"Yes," he replied. "Look here, Sylvester, old fellow, I'm sure there's something wrong at home that I don't quite understand. Mr. Denny, our lawyer, has been there with my mother, and they haven't told me what is the matter, but they seem to be afraid of something or somebody, and I believe it's Uncle Nicholas."

"Why? has he shown any signs of ill-will?"

"No; if anything, he's appeared more friendly than he has been since I can remember. He came over to Coverthorne the day after the funeral, and said he was sorry that he and my father had quarrelled; that there had probably been mistakes on both sides, but he was glad now to think that all the misunderstanding had been cleared away before James's death, and that they had mutually agreed the past should be forgiven and forgotten. My uncle must have noticed the surprised look on my mother's face, as she knew of no such reconciliation; and he went on to explain that he and my father had agreed not to make it public till next Christmas Day, when they intended to dine together. 'There's another matter which was to have been mentioned then,' he went on. 'I won't broach the subject now. After the terrible shock, you aren't in a fit state to be bothered with business. We'll leave it for a few weeks.'"

"I must say I didn't like the look of that man when I saw him," I muttered; "his face seemed hard and cruel."

"My mother mistrusts him too, and so does Mr. Denny. I can tell that by the way in which they speak about him."

For some moments Miles remained silent, scraping patterns in the gravel with the heel of his boot.

"Look here. You're an old friend whom I know I can trust, Sylvester," he exclaimed suddenly. "I'm sure if I tell you what I think you won't let it go any farther?"

I at once gave him the promise he desired.

"Soon after Uncle Nicholas's visit," he began, "Mr. Denny came to stay with us for three days, spending most of his time going through my father's papers. My mother would be closeted with him for an hour at a time. I could hear their voices talking together in low tones as I passed the door; and when they came out there was always a worried, anxious look on their faces. I had heard it mentioned that my father's will and some other documents were missing; but hitherto Mr. Denny had not treated the loss as a very serious thing, at all events as far as I could gather. I don't think I should have troubled my head any more about the matter, but for what I am going to describe. It was on the last day of Mr. Denny's visit. I had gone to bed rather early, as I was tired, and had been asleep some hours, when I was awakened by a sound like a muffled knocking. I lay for a few minutes, thinking it must have been my fancy; then the sound was repeated. The thought occurred to me at once that it must be some one who had come to the house for some reason or other, and was knocking at the back door to try and waken one of the servants. I got up, leaned out of my window, and called out, 'Who's there?' No reply was given, nor could I see any one in the yard. Once more I thought my fancy had deceived me; then *thump—thump—thump!* it came again. 'It must be some one at the front door,' I thought; so I threw a coat over my shoulders and went out of my room, down a passage, and across the landing to a window that looks out on the front of the house. I opened it, and once more asked who was there, but got no answer.

"The horses in the stables often make curious noises at night, but this rapping was too regular to have been caused by them. I walked slowly back, and just as I reached the middle of the landing it came again, *knock—knock—knock!* I expect you'll think me a coward, but I must own that a chill went all down my back. People say that Coverthorne is haunted, and this strange rapping in the middle of the night, long after every one else had gone to bed, reminded me of all the stories I had often heard the servants telling each other round the kitchen fire. If you'll believe me, I was more than half inclined to bolt for my room and stick my head under the bedclothes. The sound came from somewhere downstairs, and, as far as I could judge, from the direction of the very room which is supposed to be particularly favoured by the ghost. It was like some one rapping slowly and deliberately with his knuckles on the panel of a door. I stood irresolute and holding my breath; then I heard something tinkle like metal falling on stone. That seemed to break the spell, and my heart beat fast. I no longer feared a ghost, but thought it must be robbers. What I intended doing I hardly know, but I think I must have had some vague idea of trying to slip across the kitchen to the servants' quarters, and there rouse the men. I went slowly and carefully down the stairs, my bare feet making no sound. The knocking was repeated. I could tell now exactly from what part of the house it came, and a strong desire seized me to get a sight of the thieves and see what they were about. Old houses like ours have all kinds of funny twists and turns. I crept along to one of these, and peeped round the corner. What I saw astonished me more than if I had been confronted by a whole band of robbers. I was looking down a long, narrow passage, the walls of which are panelled with oak: at the farther end stood my mother and Mr. Denny. She was carrying a candle, while he held in his hands a hammer and small chisel; the latter it was which he must have dropped a few moments before, when I heard the chink of its fall on the flagstones. What they were doing I could not imagine. I saw Mr. Denny rap on the wall with the handle of the hammer, at the same time turning his ear to listen, as though he almost expected some one on the other side of the panelling to say 'Come in!' Then it dawned on me in a moment that they were searching for the secret place."

Miles paused as he said this, and I listened breathlessly for what was coming next.

"Of course," continued my companion, "I guessed at once that my mother and Mr. Denny were searching then, instead of in the daytime, because they thought it best for the servants not to see and go gossiping in the village. As they evidently did not want me with them, I turned and crept quietly back to bed again; but I couldn't help lying awake listening for the tap of the hammer, and from that I knew they continued searching most of the night. Try as I would, I could not rest till my curiosity was in some measure satisfied;

so on the following day, after Mr. Denny had gone back home, I told my mother what I knew, and begged her to give me an explanation. Even then she wouldn't tell me plainly what was the matter. She said Mr. Denny had heard a rumour which made him uneasy about our future, and that he wanted to find some letters and papers which he thought it possible my father might have stowed away in the secret place. She warned me to be sure and not mention this to the servants, and, above all, to Uncle Nicholas."

My companion's story reawakened all the former interest which I had felt in the old house. It seemed to me a place which must be abounding in mystery, and almost as romantic as the enchanted castle of a fairy tale.

"I *should* like to help to search, and see if I couldn't find the secret place," I blurted out.

"So you shall," answered Miles. "It was understood that you were to stay with me at Coverthorne." Then seeing that I hesitated, regretful at having reminded him of a promise which had been made before the sad circumstance of his father's death—"Oh yes," he added, "I'm quite expecting you to come back with me. Mother wishes it too, for she thinks it will do me good to have some companion of my own age, to cheer me up. It will be fine," he went on, his face growing brighter than I had seen it since his return to the school. "We'll shoot rabbits, and bathe, and go down to Rockymouth, and go fishing in one of the boats. There'll be heaps to do, if only we get fine weather."

All these projects were delightful to contemplate, but the thought of searching for that mysterious hidden chamber was what still appealed most strongly to my imagination.

"What a pity your father wasn't able to tell you the secret before you came of age!" I remarked.

"I daresay he would have," answered Miles sadly, "if only I had arrived in time to see him alive."

"Haven't you been able to find any clue that would help you in the search?"

"No; the secret has been so well kept, and handed on from father to son, that, outside our family, many people who have heard the story think there is no such place."

"Has it ever been used for anything?"

"Not that I know of, except, I believe, years ago. When there was the scare of a French invasion, my grandfather, who was alive then, hid all his silver and valuables there. About a year ago my father went to London, and Mr. Denny thinks it possible that before he started he might have wanted to find a safe place for his papers, put them in the secret chamber, and not troubled to take them out again when he came back."

It seems to me that in my young days the prospect of breaking up and going home for the holidays was a period which occasioned a greater amount of rejoicing and excitement than it does among the younger generation of the present time. For one thing, the contrast between school and home was greater then; and again, the half-year was longer than the term, and the end of it the more eagerly awaited. Now, my grandchildren appear to be no sooner packed off to school than they are back again. In addition to all this, when that particular vacation drew near, the prospect of returning home with Miles for a fortnight at Coverthorne made me long all the more for the few remaining days to pass; and when at length we flung our dog-eared school books into our desks for the last time, and rushed out into the playground to give vent to our feelings with three rousing cheers, I know I shouted till I was hoarse.

Owing to the limited accommodation on the coaches, we had two actual breaking-up days—half of the boys going home on the one and half on the other, those whose progress in school work had been most satisfactory being allowed to start first.

Miles and I had the good fortune to be numbered among the latter, and I don't think I shall ever forget that bright summer morning when, together with several more companions, we started to walk to the little village of Round Green, through which the coach passed about nine o'clock. Our luggage had already preceded us in a cart, to be transferred to the boot of the *Regulator*, the guard of which, George Woodley by name, was a prime favourite with us boys.

Shutting my eyes for a moment, I can imagine myself standing again outside the Sportsman Inn at Round Green, waiting with boyish eagerness for the first distant note of the horn which—this being the end of a stage—was sounded to give the hostlers warning to bring out the fresh horses. What music ever was so sweet on a bright summer morning as that gay call, coupled with the brisk clattering of the hoofs, when it sounded in the ears of a boy returning home from school? How we held our breath and strained our ears to listen for the approaching vehicle! I could almost imagine I heard that far-off fanfare now, forgetful of the fact that the gulf of a long life divides me from that time, that the railway has long displaced the *Regulator*, and that coachman, guard, and most of their young passengers know now a greater secret than the one which, during the coming holidays, I hoped to fathom.

CHAPTER III.

MEN IN HIDING.

When in actual sight of the two things I had most longed to see, I can hardly say which of them more strongly attracted my attention—the sea glistening like a sheet of silver in the distance, or the old house nestling down among the trees, with its mullioned windows, gray, lichen-covered walls, and the funny little cupola surmounting the roof, and containing the bell which was rung to summon the farm hands to their meals. The coach had put us down at a spot on the highroad known as Tod's Corner, where an old servant had met us, and driven us the rest of the way in a light trap which was just large enough to hold us and our luggage.

Even at the first glance Coverthorne quite realized my expectations. The house and farm buildings formed a quadrangle, while the windows of the sitting-rooms looked out into a quiet, old walled garden, with fruit-trees, box-edged paths, beds of old-fashioned flowers, and a big mulberry tree, in the shade of which was a rustic seat. Inside the building was a large stone-flagged hall, in which, except on special occasions, we had our meals. The rooms were low and cool, the steps of the staircase were shallow and broad, flanked with a ponderous balustrade of dark oak, while panelling of the same material covered the walls of the best rooms and some of the passages. The whole place seemed characteristic of a peaceful old age, and it was almost impossible to think that within its walls anything could ever occur to disturb its restful quiet with any jarring note of violence or fear.

Mrs. Coverthorne gave me a kindly welcome, though it was evident that she had not yet recovered from the shock of her husband's death. Her quiet voice and motherly smile at once won my affections; but often, when her face was in

23

repose, it bore a sad and harassed expression which did not escape my notice, and which brought back to my mind a remembrance of the hints which Miles had given me at school, of some trouble, in addition to his father's death, which overshadowed the family.

We arrived early in the afternoon, and after a hearty meal, for which the long ride in the fresh air had given us an appetite, we hurried out of doors, to go the round of the place, and visit all Miles's favourite haunts. To the neighbouring pond and water-wheel, the orchard, the stables and dog-kennels—to these and a score of other places my friend rushed, eager to discover whether any changes had taken place; and after he had satisfied his curiosity on these points, we went farther afield, roaming over the estate, which on that side included all the land between Coverthorne and the sea. In those days, when people did comparatively little travelling, the sight of the ocean was more of a novelty to an inland-bred boy than it would be now; and standing on the summit of a headland, listening to the surging of the waves against the foot of the precipice over which we gazed, I caught my breath, thrilled with a feeling which was almost one of awe. Away to our left was the little coast village of Rockymouth, and as we looked we could see a tiny fishing-boat beating up against the wind to make the harbour, while on either hand the formidable line of frowning cliffs stretched away, headland beyond headland, till lost in the blue and hazy distance. To me the view was like a scene from some stirring romance, and I drank it in, little thinking under what different circumstances I should one day renew my acquaintance with that sea and shore.

So many things there were to occupy our attention during that first afternoon and evening that, for the time being, our resolve to search for the secret place was banished from our minds; but after we had finished breakfast on the following morning, I reminded Miles of our project.

"D'you want to begin at once?" he asked, smiling.

"Why not!" I returned; "it won't take us long."

"Won't it?" answered my companion. "Don't you be so cocksure till you've tried.—By the way," he continued, his face changing from gay to grave, "we'd better not let my mother know what we're doing; it would only revive unpleasant thoughts in her mind."

"Would she be vexed if she found out we were searching for the hiding-place?" I asked.

"Oh no! it's the loss of the papers she troubles so much about."

It was easy to make an excuse for wandering about the house, and together we examined every nook and corner, from the cold, gloomy cellars to dark and stuffy holes in the roof. More than once I thought I had made some wonderful discovery when I came across mysterious little doors in some of the bedrooms opening into dark cupboards or closets in the wall; but Miles in every case damped my enthusiasm by saying that these were already well known to the whole household. I must confess that in my own mind I had fondly imagined I should discover the secret chamber without much difficulty, but soon I began to realize that it was not such an easy task as I had expected, and at the end of a couple of hours I came near to owning myself beaten.

"This is where I saw old Denny sounding the walls with the hammer," said Miles. As my companion spoke, we were passing down the narrow wainscoted passage which he had described to me at school. I struck the boarding myself once or twice with my knuckles as we moved along, but produced no sound which might betoken the presence of a hollow cavity behind the oak. Arriving at length at an old square-panelled doorway, we entered a room which I at once realized I had not been inside before. Save for a plain wooden chair and table, it was empty and destitute of furniture. There was nothing specially remarkable about the place, yet the appearance of its interior seems so vividly impressed on my mind, that I can see it now as though at this moment I were once more crossing the threshold.

The apartment was evidently intended for a sort of morning room or second parlour. The walls were panelled with oak, and a carved mantelpiece, of massive though not elaborate design, framed the wide, open hearth. There was a curious earthy smell about the place, probably owing to the fact that it was never used; which seemed strange, for it had a pleasant outlook into the garden.

"What a jolly room!" I exclaimed. "Why isn't it used?"

Miles gave a short laugh.

"There's no need," he answered; "we've got enough without it."

We crossed the bare floor and sat down in the deep window-seat. I still went on talking, but, though I hardly noticed it at the time, my companion grew quieter than before. He returned absent-minded replies to my questions, and seemed, from the position of his head, as though he half expected to hear something in the passage or the garden. We may have sat like this for ten minutes or longer, when suddenly an intent expression on Miles's face caused me to break off abruptly in what I was saying. Then, for the first time, I became aware of a curious sound, faint and subdued, as though some one were humming with the mouth closed. At first it seemed far away; then it might have been in the room, though in what part it was impossible to say. I was listening idly and with no particular wonder to the noise, when Miles rose to his feet.

"Come on," he said abruptly.

For a moment I hesitated, not understanding this sudden move; then seeing my friend already half-way across the room, I rose and followed.

"Where are you going?" I asked.

"Oh, anywhere," he answered, almost snappishly, and I wondered what could have upset his temper.

A boy's thoughts turn quickly from one point to another, like a weather-vane in a changing wind, and that afternoon our search for the secret chamber was abandoned in favour of another form of amusement. Miles had already learned to shoot, and promised to take me out with him that evening in the hope that we might get a few rabbits. I was, of course, eager for the expedition, though my own part in it would be the comparatively humble one of carrying the flasks for powder and shot. What a clumsy thing that old flintlock fowling-piece would appear now beside the modern breechloader! Yet how I envied my friend its possession while I watched him cleaning it, as we sat in the garden, sheltered from the hot sun by the thick foliage of the old mulberry tree!

"There!" said Miles at length, as he threw aside the oiled rag and brought the weapon to his shoulder; "with a charge well rammed home, I'll warrant her to kill as far as any gun in the county!"

The heat of the day was past when we set out, and the landscape appeared bathed in warm evening sunshine. I wished that the "Foxes" and "Eagles" could see us sallying forth armed with a real gun; and when about two fields away from the house we halted to load and prime the piece, I felt almost as though I were actually embarked on one of the wild adventures of the hunter heroes of our Indian tales.

As far as actual sport went, we tramped a long way with very little result. We should see rabbits feeding out in the fields as we crept up under the hedges, but before we got within range they would suddenly prick up their ears and scamper back to their holes.

"The ground is so hard in this hot weather that they hear us coming," muttered Miles; but he managed to get a few shots, and, much to my delight, killed two, which he handed to me to carry.

So we went on, walking across the open, or creeping cautiously along under the shadow of hedges and bushes, until we reached the summit of the cliffs, where we sat down to rest.

"How many ships can you see?" asked Miles.

"Two," I replied.

"I can make out a third!" he answered, pointing with his finger. "My eyes, I expect, are sharper than yours. It's a great deal a matter of practice. You'd be surprised what keen sight some of the men have here who've been sailors. Old Lewis, for instance—he can tell a ship's nationality when she appears only a speck on the horizon, and I believe he can see almost as well in the dark as he can in the daylight. He's a curious old fellow. Some afternoon we'll go out fishing with him in his boat."

We sat looking out over the vast expanse of ocean till the sun sank like a huge ball of fire below the horizon; then my companion rose once more to his feet.

"It's time we went back to supper," he said, "or mother will be getting anxious, and think we've met with an accident. She's been very nervous since father's death."

Crossing a stretch of common land, we found ourselves looking down on a little sheltered valley, through which ran a tiny stream, winding its way towards a little cove where I knew my friend often went to bathe. Worn out, no doubt, in the course of ages by the water, this gully narrowed down as it neared the sea, but where we stood it was some little distance across, and the farther side was covered with quite a thick copse of trees and bushes.

"I wish I'd brought the dog with me," said Miles. "There is any quantity of rabbits here. Still, we may be able to get a shot. If we creep along till we reach that corner," he continued, as we entered the fringe of the wood, "we may find some of them sitting out in the open."

Bending down, we moved forward in single file, avoiding any dry twigs which might crack beneath our feet. In this manner we had proceeded some distance, when I was startled by a rustling in the bushes, and a big brown dog went bounding across our path.

"You poaching rascal!" exclaimed Miles, and raised his gun to his shoulder. He was, I am sure, too kind-hearted to have actually shot the dog; it was more of an angry gesture, or he might have intended to send the charge a few yards behind the animal's tail to give it a fright. Anyway, before he could have had time to pull the trigger, to my astonishment a man suddenly rose up close to us, as though out of the ground.

"Don't shoot, Master Miles!" he cried. "It be only old Joey, and he's doing no harm."

The speaker was clad in a dilapidated hat, a blue jersey, and a pair of old trousers stuffed into a fisherman's boots. I set him down at once as a poacher, and was astonished at the friendly tone in which he addressed the owner of the property on which he was found trespassing. I was still further surprised when Miles, instead of showing any signs of resentment, merely turned and said in an almost jocular tone,—

"Hullo! what are you up to? It's a mercy I didn't mistake you for a fox or a rabbit, and put a charge of shot into your whiskers."

"Just out for an evening stroll, sir, and lay down to rest," replied the man, whistling the dog to his side. There was a funny twinkle in his piercing gray eyes as he spoke, the meaning of which Miles seemed to fathom, for his own face relaxed into a grin.

"Begging your pardon, sir," the fellow continued, "I don't think you're likely to find any rabbits in this copse to-night. They're all gone to bed early, or perhaps old Joey may have frightened them."

For another moment Miles and the man stood looking into each other's faces, and once more the meaning smile passed between them; then the former uncocked his gun, and slung it over his shoulder.

There was a funny twinkle in his eyes as he spoke.

"All right!" he answered.—"Come on, Sylvester; it's time we went back to supper."

There was no hedge to the copse. We stepped out from among the trees and underwood, and had not gone far when the man came running after us.

"Master Miles," he said, "if ever you want to go a-fishing, you can come down to Rockymouth and have the boat, sir; and if you'll give me a call, I'll go with you."

I hardly heard what he said, for glancing into the wood, something caught my eye which immediately riveted my attention. Projecting from behind a clump of bushes were a pair of heavy boots, and as I looked one of them moved, which showed conclusively that they were not empty. I waited till we had got some little distance beyond the copse, and then seized my companion's arm.

"Miles," I whispered, "there's another man hiding in the wood."

"Is there?" he answered carelessly. "Some friend of old Lewis, I suppose."

"Is that the old sailor you were talking about?" I asked. "What's he doing in your wood at this time in the evening? Lying down, too, concealed among the bushes. He must be poaching."

Miles only smiled, and shook his head.

"He's all right. The chap wouldn't harm a stick of our property; in fact, he'd just about murder any one who did."

Though more mystified than ever with this explanation, it was the only one I could get, and we walked on talking of other matters until we came within a field of the house. The darkness had almost fallen by this time, though back across the undulating country I could just see the dark ridge where the tree tops rose above the side of the valley.

"I'm going to fire," said Miles; "it saves the bother of drawing the charge."

The report of the piece rang out, and echoed over the quiet country, and as though in answer to the sound there

31

came out of the distance the sharp bark of a dog. It was evident that the man Lewis was still enjoying his evening stroll in the wood.

"Master Joe's getting out of training, I fancy," muttered Miles, as though speaking to himself. "I say," he added aloud, "you needn't mention anything to mother about our meeting those men in the wood. They aren't up to any harm, but it might make her more nervous; she gets frightened at anything now."

"But what are they doing?" I asked. "Surely they can't be loitering out there for fun?"

Miles laughed.

"It's fun of a sort," he answered. "I'll tell you some day. Now come on in to supper."

It was one of those hot, still nights when it seems impossible to sleep, and tired though I was with my long ramble in the open air, I lay tossing from side to side, now and again dozing off into an uneasy slumber, only to once more suddenly find myself broad awake. At length, feeling very thirsty, I got up and groped my way across to the washstand for a drink of water. A delicious cool breeze had just begun to come in at the window. I went over and leaned out. The sky was gray and wan with the first pale light of dawn, and the country over which I gazed looked ghostly and strange in the twilight. With my arms folded on the sill, I remained for some time drawing in the fresh morning air in deep breaths, and fascinated by the solemn silence which still reigned over the sleeping world, when to my ear came suddenly an unexpected sound—the clatter of a closing gate.

Wondering who could be about at that early hour, I gazed across the neighbouring field, and so doing saw the figures of two men emerge from the deep shadow of the farthest hedge. At a peculiar jog-trot they crossed the open till a slope in the ground once more hid them from my view. The light was not strong enough to allow of my making out anything beyond the outline of their figures, but it seemed to me that each carried on his back something which I thought resembled a soldier's knapsack. It was impossible, I say, for me to recognize their faces, but following close at the heels of the first I distinctly saw a dog, and immediately decided in my own mind that the man must be Lewis, whom I had seen a few hours before hiding in the wood. What the men could be doing, or whither they were going, I had not the faintest idea, but it struck me that they were up to no good, and that their errand was one which they would not have performed in broad daylight. No other person crossed the field, and at length, greatly perplexed, I returned to bed.

I began to think there were other mysteries to be solved at Coverthorne besides the whereabouts of the secret chamber.

CHAPTER IV.

THE SINGING GHOST.

Though I longed to tell Miles of what I had seen in the early morning, yet on second thoughts I decided to let the matter drop. The vague replies which he had given to my questions of the previous evening showed clearly that he was not disposed to give me a true explanation of the fisherman's presence in the wood. I must own that this puzzled me not a little, for, certain as I felt of my comrade's uprightness and honour, it was firmly impressed on my mind that there was something very questionable in old Lewis's conduct; and if this were so, it was difficult to understand why Miles should tolerate underhand doings on what was now practically his own estate. It was, however, after all, no business of mine; and I determined to restrain my curiosity till my friend chose to explain, or a good opportunity occurred for me to broach the subject again, and ask him further questions.

At odd times we continued our search for the secret place, but without any further success than before. Miles became inclined to treat the matter as a joke, but I had some reason to believe that, though our search and the various incidents connected with it were often highly amusing, the loss of the papers, which it was possible had been placed in the hidden chamber, might prove more serious than my school friend fully understood.

What suggested this thought to my mind was part of a conversation which I chanced to overhear under circumstances which were briefly as follows. On about the fourth day of my visit Mr. Denny put in an appearance at the house. I did not know of his arrival, but on going into the parlour for something I found him there with Mrs. Coverthorne, turning out the contents of an old bureau which stood against the wall. I merely entered the room and went out again, but that was long enough for me to see that not only were the table and the window-seat littered with the contents of pigeonholes and drawers, but that all the books had been removed from the shelves above, and were undergoing a careful examination, as though it were thought possible that some paper of importance might be found between their leaves.

At dinner I sat opposite the lawyer. He was a thin, dry little man, with very bright eyes and quick, jerky movements which reminded me of a bird. He spoke kindly to us boys, cracked jokes, and spoke about our school life and our holiday amusements; but in spite of this I could not help thinking that his gaiety was rather forced. Mrs. Coverthorne, too, looked more anxious than usual; and though she also made attempts to be cheerful, I felt sure that the lawyer's business with her had not been of a pleasant or reassuring nature.

Almost directly after the meal was finished Miles started off on an errand to Rockymouth—Mr. Denny, who lived there, having arranged to return later in the afternoon. Left to myself, I climbed into the old mulberry tree, and discovering a most comfortable perch among the branches, read a book until I fell asleep.

As a combined result of the strong sea air and an unusual amount of outdoor exercise, I must have slept pretty soundly; but I was at length aroused by the sound of voices, and looking down through the leafy branches saw Mrs. Coverthorne and the lawyer walking down the garden path towards the gate. They did not see me, and I could not help overhearing what they said, though the only words which reached my ears were those which they spoke as they were passing close to the tree.

"Don't be too downhearted, ma'am," Mr. Denny was saying in his brisk manner; "there's still that one chance I spoke of. We haven't had an opportunity to compare the dates yet, and that's an important matter."

"I cannot bring myself to think it possible that my dear husband could have done such a thing—at least without telling me of his intentions. There must be some great mistake. We mustn't tell Miles, not just yet, for I had so wished to make these holidays specially happy."

A few moments later, as the speaker was returning alone to the house, I saw that she was weeping. A great longing filled my heart to understand her trouble, and to render her and Miles some assistance. It seemed a vain and hopeless wish, for of what use could I, a mere schoolboy and comparative stranger, possibly be to them? Yet the unexpected often happens, and the queer cross-currents on the sea of life bring about unlooked-for meetings with equally strange results.

Two days later a respectable working-man made his appearance at Coverthorne. We heard that he was a master-builder, and that he had come to give some advice about repairs. He went all over the house, even going so far as to climb more than half-way up two of the big chimneys. It was, I say, given out that he was to ascertain whether certain of the walls and parts of the roof needed repair, but I hazarded a shrewd guess that he had been employed by Mr. Denny in a confidential manner to apply his practical knowledge of building and architecture in a further attempt to find the secret chamber. If this were so, the man was not any more successful than we boys had been. Granted that such a hiding-place really existed, it was constructed in some most unlikely place, or concealed in an unusually skilful manner.

Miles and I sought it again more than once; but gradually, when the novelty of the idea had worn off and the quest appeared hopeless, I must confess that I began to lose interest in the matter, and to devote my attention to more attractive amusements.

There was certainly no lack of these at Coverthorne. We shot rabbits, bathed from the beach of the little sheltered cove, and went out to sea and fished for whiting and pollack. In pursuit of this last-named form of sport we usually made use of a boat which belonged to the man Lewis. He seemed very willing for us to have it, often came out with us himself, teaching us how to row and to use the sail, and refusing to accept any money in return.

In addition to the fact of having seen him under circumstances which naturally excited my curiosity, there was something about the man which roused my interest in a special degree. As a boy he had served in the navy, having been present at the battle of the Nile; and how eagerly we listened to accounts of those great fights with the French on sea and land, the memory of which was still fresh in men's minds when I was a lad! The brown dog almost always accompanied its master. It was a very intelligent animal, and however far from home, if given anything and told to carry it back to its master's cottage, it would do so with the greatest certainty and promptitude.

Though past middle age, and round-shouldered like many old sailors, Lewis was wonderfully active, and sprang from one boat to another in the harbour or climbed the rocks with the agility of a cat. It was really this which, by accident, led to my making some further discoveries with regard to the old salt. We had been out for a sail, and Lewis, after taking leave of us, was running along the village street to overtake some friend whom he saw in the distance.

"The old beggar can cover the ground at a good pace still," remarked Miles.

"I saw him from my bedroom window the other night," I remarked unthinkingly, "cutting across your field with something which looked like a soldier's knapsack on his back. He must have a good wind."

"Soldier's knapsack!" blurted out Miles with a laugh. "More like a keg of French brandy, with another on his chest to keep the balance."

"What?" I exclaimed.

Taken off his guard, Miles had gone a bit too far to refuse a further explanation.

"I don't suppose it matters if I tell you," he remarked, with a glance over his shoulder to make sure that no one else was listening. "Old Lewis goes in a bit for what used to be known as the 'free trade,' but what you now hear of as smuggling."

"I thought smugglers were men who owned ships and sailed across from France with tobacco, and lace, and spirits—" I began.

"So they do," interrupted Miles; "but there are smugglers on land as well as on sea. The men who bring the stuff across from France only do part of the work; when it is put ashore it has to be taken inland and sold, and often it has to be hidden away somewhere till the preventive men are off their guard. Bless you, I know all about it, and you would too if you'd lived as long as I have on the coast."

"And was that what he was up to the night we found him in the little wood by the cliffs?" I asked, a light suddenly breaking in on my mind.

"Yes," answered Miles. "I saw at a glance what was afoot. You noticed another man hiding behind a bush. I daresay there were a dozen more of them in the copse."

"But what were they doing there?"

"Well, it would take a long time to explain it all in detail: but to put it in a few words, what happens is something like this. Somebody—probably old Lewis or another man— arranges with the owner of a lugger to bring some brandy from France, the spirit being sent over in little tubs or ankers. It is, of course, all arranged beforehand just when and where the stuff is to be landed, and preparations are made accordingly. Lewis gets a number of men, farm labourers and others, to act as what are termed 'carriers,' and these meet and lie hidden somewhere close to the place on the coast where the run is to take place. The tubs are all fastened to a long rope, so that, as soon as ever the lugger brings to, the end of this rafting line can be conveyed to the beach, and the whole 'crop' dragged on shore. With the same cords by which the tubs are fastened to the ropes they are then tied together in such a way that the carriers can sling them over their shoulders. Each man takes two ankers, and then they scatter, and dash off inland to some meeting-place already agreed upon. In this way, when the men are up to their work, it takes only a few minutes for the lugger to discharge her cargo, while the carriers get clear of the beach and disappear."

I must own to being rather shocked at the careless and even jocular tone in which my companion described a traffic which I had always heard spoken of as a crime.

"But, Miles," I began, "it's against the law!"

"Oh, of course it is!" he answered, laughing; "but who's going to interfere with a few poor men turning a penny now and then? The only result is that people round about get better brandy than they otherwise would have done, and a good bit cheaper. Of course people like us don't have any share in the business, but when we know anything is happening we just look the other way."

The weak points in my comrade's arguments may be patent enough to the present-day reader of this story; but it is due to him to say that in those times, especially along the coast, defrauding the revenue was hardly looked upon as a crime, and in the still earlier times of "free trade" this idea had an even greater hold on the minds of the common people, who were always ready to regard the smuggler as a hero, and the exciseman as a villain. Old ideas die hard in country places, and Miles had listened to the talk of the fisher folk since childhood, and had been accustomed to regard the matter from their point of view.

I had always imagined the smuggler as a picturesque sort of villain, sailing the seas in a saucy craft, with a belt stuck full of knives and pistols, and I must own to something like a feeling of disappointment when brought face to face with the original.

"Don't they ever have fights with the coast-guards?" I asked.

"Not if they can help it," was the reply. "You see if they resisted and wounded the officers it would be a serious thing, and might mean transportation for some of them. There's been a lively chase once or twice. I'm very much afraid, though, that there'll be an ugly row some day if they are caught; for old Lewis and some of his men are determined fellows, and as likely as not would show fight before allowing their kegs to be taken."

The remainder of the way home was beguiled with further tales of the doings of the smugglers.

"Look here," Miles concluded, as we came in sight of the house. "Of course mother doesn't know all this, or I expect she'd object to our going out so much with Lewis. All I do is what I did the other night: if I know the men are on our ground, I look the other way. It's no business of mine to meddle with their doings, and there isn't one of them who would take a single rabbit or forget to shut a gate behind him. If he did, he'd soon hear of it from the others."

The remainder of my stay at Coverthorne passed pleasantly if uneventfully, nothing of any note happening until the last day of my visit, when an incident occurred which I have good reason always to remember.

The day was wet and stormy. Miles was engaged doing something for his mother, and having nothing particular with which to occupy my attention, I strolled from one part of the house to another, and at length found my way to the empty room which I have already described, and which I discovered by this time was spoken of as the west parlour. This morning the curious earthy smell which I had remarked there before seemed stronger than usual; but in spite of this and its bare and neglected appearance, the room struck me as one which would have been pleasant and cosy if properly furnished.

I strolled over to the window-seat, and sat gazing round at the dark oak panelling, wondering vaguely why the place was never used. If occupied in no other way, it surprised me that Miles did not appropriate it for a sort of private den or workshop. I was lolling back, idly poking a straw into a crevice of the woodwork, when suddenly the same strange sound broke on my ear which I had heard before. I sat up to listen. It was like some one humming without any regard to tune. At one time it seemed to come from a distant part of the house, and then it appeared to be actually in the room.

One glance was sufficient to show that the chamber itself was empty. I listened with awakened curiosity, but with no sensation of uneasiness or fear. What could it be?

Rising to my feet I walked across the room, stepped into the open fireplace, and stared up the wide chimney. Some spots of rain fell on my upturned face, but nothing was to be seen except the gray sky overhead. I stepped back into the room, and still the muffled drone continued, rising and falling, and then ceasing altogether.

"It must be the wind in the chimney," I thought, and moved once more into the open hearth; but now the sound seemed in the room, and was certainly not in the stone shaft above my head. I next opened the window and looked out into the walled garden. No noise, however, was to be heard there but the patter of the raindrops on the leaves of the trees. Perplexed and rather astonished, I now crossed the floor, opened the door, and went out into the passage, only to find it empty. Once more, as I stood undecided what to do next, the crooning notes fell on my ear, and I began to think that some one was playing me a trick. It was just as I had arrived at this conclusion that I heard Miles calling me; and a moment later, in obedience to my answering hail, he joined me in the empty room.

"I keep hearing that funny noise," I said, "and I can't make out where it comes from."

He made no reply, but stood at my side listening till the sound came again, this time a long, mournful wail like that of some one in pain. I turned, and was surprised to find that Miles's face was almost bloodless. He slipped his arm within mine, and drew me towards the door.

"What can it be?" I asked.

"No one will ever know for certain," he answered, speaking almost in a whisper. "The room is haunted!"

"Haunted!" I cried, stopping short as I gained the passage. "You don't believe in ghosts?"

"I believe in that one," he answered. "I've heard it too often to have any doubt. That's the reason we never use the room; only mother doesn't like it talked about, because it only frightens the servants. People have tried to make out it was the wind; but though we've blocked up the chimney, and have stopped every crack and hole we could find, it makes no difference to the sound, and no one can tell from what part of the room it comes. Besides, the story is that my great-grandfather died there. When he was an old man he always went about humming to himself, and making just the same sort of noise that has been heard in the room ever since his death. All the people round know about it, and they call it the Singing Ghost of Coverthorne."

"O Miles," I began, "you don't believe such stuff as that?"

"I know you'll think me a coward," he interrupted. "I'm not afraid of most things, but I own frankly I hate to go near that horrid room. Mother had it furnished, and tried to use it one winter; but at the end of a month she got so frightened of the noise that she declared she'd never sit there again."

"I don't mind your ghost," I exclaimed, laughing. "You wait here, and I'll go back and listen to it again."

I entered the room, closed the door behind me, and stood waiting in a corner of the floor. I tried to persuade myself that I was not in the least frightened, but my heart beat faster than usual, and I strained my ears with almost painful intentness to catch the slightest sound. Within the last few moments the place seemed to have grown more cold, damp, and earthy than before; it felt like standing in a vault. Then, whether from the floor, ceiling, or solid oak panelling on the walls, I could not tell, came once more that mysterious sound, as though a person were humming with closed lips. I cast one hasty glance round the room, and made hurriedly for the door. Miles was still waiting in the passage.

"You didn't stay very long," he remarked with a quiet smile.

CHAPTER V.

NICHOLAS COVERTHORNE SHOWS HIS HAND.

In due course the summer holidays came to an end, and Miles and I met again at school. I had not been in his company five minutes before I noticed that his face wore a different look from when I had seen him last at Coverthorne; indeed, he seemed once more as sad and dejected as he had appeared immediately after his father's funeral.

"What's the matter with you? Have you been ill?" I asked; but he only shook his head and gave evasive replies.

The first day of the half was always one of excitement. The reunion of old friends, the appearance of new boys and masters, the changes of classes and dormitories, all aroused our lively interest; but Miles seemed in no mood to join in our fun. He slipped out of the playground as soon as work was finished, and went off for a walk alone.

Thinking that his return to school had in some way recalled the consciousness of his bereavement, I allowed him for a time to go his own way; but when tea was over I determined to find him, and at least offer him some expression of sympathy. After a little search I discovered him standing with his back against a tree moodily chewing a piece of straw.

"There is something the matter with you," I said. "Why won't you tell me? Is it private?" My arm seemed naturally to slip through his as I asked the question, and perhaps the action, simple as it was, gave him a fresh assurance of my friendship, and influenced him to unburden himself of what was on his mind.

"There's no harm in my telling you, Sylvester," he replied. "I know you won't let it go any further. I'm upset by what's happened at home."

"Something that has happened since I stayed with you?" I asked.

"Well, yes," he answered—"that is, it's come to a head since your visit. I daresay while you were with us you noticed that there was something wrong, and that my mother often seemed worried and depressed. It was not till after you'd gone that I found out what was really the matter."

He paused as though expecting me to speak, but I made no interruption.

"As I've already told you, my father made a will about two years ago," continued Miles. "He signed it at Mr. Denny's office, and took it away with him; but now it can't be found. My mother always thought that it was in the secret drawer of the bureau; but it proved to be empty when she went to look. Then, as I've mentioned before, the idea occurred to her and Mr. Denny that it had been put away for safety in the secret place. If that's the case, then goodness knows if either the papers or the hidden chamber will ever be discovered. At least so far all attempts have proved a failure. Mr. Denny even goes so far as to suggest that the so-called hiding-place may be nothing but a small cavity in the wall behind some sliding panel; though he admits that, from a remark he once heard my father make, he had always believed it was a place large enough to conceal a man. If it's only a little hole somewhere in the stonework, we might pull the house down before we found it."

"But see here," I interrupted. "I don't understand anything about lawyers' business; but even if your father's will were lost, I suppose the property will come to you all the same, seeing that you are his only son."

"Wait a moment till I have finished the story," continued my companion. "When I talked to you about this once before, I described how my uncle came to Coverthorne soon after my father's funeral, and spoke to my mother about a secret reconciliation between the brothers, and hinted at a matter of business which he would discuss at some future time, when she should have recovered somewhat from the shock of her loss. My mother was surprised, and thought it very strange, as she had heard no word from her husband to lead her to suppose that he had made up the quarrel with his brother. The matter, I say, puzzled her a good bit, but did not cause her any actual uneasiness till Mr. Denny came one day and told her privately of an extraordinary rumour he had heard in Rockymouth, to the effect that Uncle Nicholas had told some one that my father had made a will leaving him half the property, that being the fair share which he ought to have had after my grandfather's death. This rumour, coupled with what my uncle had already said to her, caused my mother to begin to fear that something was wrong. She wanted to write to Uncle Nicholas right away; but Mr. Denny advised her to say nothing till she heard from him. In the meantime they made further attempts to find the will which my father had signed in the lawyer's office, Mr. Denny knowing the terms of this one, and hoping it would bear a more recent date than any other which my father might have made. You see, if a man makes more than one will it's the last that counts, and the others are worth nothing."

I nodded to show that I understood this explanation.

"About a week or ten days after you left," went on Miles, "one afternoon Uncle Nicholas called, and out came the whole affair. He produced the will of which we had already heard the rumour, and said that my father had executed it at the time that they had made up their quarrel. The terms were exactly what Mr. Denny had already hinted—that if my father died first, half the estate was to go to Nicholas; in case, however, Nicholas did not survive his brother, the whole property would come to my mother and myself. Having read the paper, he once more described how my father had been prompted to take this step out of a sense of justice; and then he added that, after all, it would make very little difference to any of us, since he himself had no children, and I should be his heir. He would only enjoy his share during the rest of his life, which at most would not be many years. From the first my mother was amazed and incensed at this disclosure. Though she saw the signature at the foot of the document, and recognized it as my father's handwriting, yet she could not but regard the whole thing as an unfair and wicked attempt on my uncle's part to rob us of our possessions. My father had been so open in his dealings, and she had always shared his confidence; it seemed, therefore, almost impossible that he should have taken such a step without at least telling her of his intentions. The interview soon became a stormy one. Uncle Nicholas, in a cold, half-ironical manner, said he felt sure that my mother would not oppose her dead husband's wishes; and gave as the reason for our not finding another will that my father had no doubt destroyed the first before making the second. He pooh-poohed the idea of any document being deposited in the hidden chamber, saying that the so-called secret place was merely a hole in one of the chimneys, which had been built up in my grandfather's time to prevent the birds building there and making a mess. My mother, however, would not be convinced, though this fresh will was clearly of a later date than the one for which she had been searching. She would not admit the justice of my uncle's claims, reminding him that he had received his portion from his father in money. She accused him of attempting to deprive his brother's widow and only son of their heritage, and at length refused to discuss the subject any further, directing him to communicate in future with our lawyer, Mr. Denny.

"'Very well,' answered my uncle shortly. 'If you are determined not to listen to reason, I can say no more; but I had much rather have settled the matter amicably between ourselves without creating a public scandal.' His face was black as thunder as he left the house, and I could see at once that all his former pleasant manners had been simply put on for the time being to suit his own purpose. Two days later

Mr. Denny called to see us, and he and my mother had a long talk in the dining-room. I wasn't present myself, but I learned afterwards that my uncle had gone straight from us to the lawyer. The latter had seen the will, and was obliged to confess that it seemed genuine and in order, and was dated at least eighteen months after the one executed at his office. I think old Denny was as much surprised at my father's conduct as my mother had been, and he questioned her closely to find out whether anything had ever happened which could in any way have brought my father into Nicholas's power, so that he might have been induced by threats of any kind to make such a disposition of his property. Of course my mother knew nothing of the kind; but in calling to mind everything she could remember, she recollected that a few months back she had seen my father address and send a large sealed envelope to his brother, and as this would have been just about the time when Nicholas asserted that the reconciliation had taken place, it seemed possible that this very letter might have contained the will. The document, I should say, was witnessed by a housekeeper of my uncle's who had since died, and by a sea captain who had often stayed at Stonebank, but whose vessel had foundered in a storm, with all hands. The fact that both of the witnesses were dead seemed suspicious, but there was no flaw in the signatures, and Nicholas had a witness who could prove that my father and Rhodes, the master-mariner, had met at Stonebank on the day the will was signed."

"Then what is going to be done?" I asked.

"What can be done?" returned Miles, with a shrug of his shoulders. "My uncle poses as a model of forbearance, and says he will allow us to remain in possession of the whole estate till the beginning of the New Year, at which date the property will be duly divided."

"At least you'll have the old house," I remarked, not knowing what else to say.

"Yes; but look here, Sylvester," my friend exclaimed. "We shall never be able to live on at Coverthorne as we're doing now if half the property is taken away from us. I believe Uncle Nicholas knows that," continued the speaker excitedly. "He wants to force us to leave, and then he'll raise or borrow money from somewhere, and so come to be owner of the whole place. He's a bad man—you can see it in his face—and how ever he induced my father to make the will I can't imagine."

"I can't either," I replied. "I disliked your uncle the first time I saw him. I believe he's a villain."

A sudden rush of boys towards the spot where we stood talking put an end to our conversation, but the substance of it was constantly recurring to my mind. I had quite made up my mind that Nicholas Coverthorne was an unscrupulous rascal, and a few days later an incident happened which not only tended to increase my dislike of the man, but to invest him and his doings with a certain sinister air of mystery.

Dr. Bagley had been expecting a parcel to be left by the coach at Round Green, and knowing that Miles was accustomed to horses, he asked him to drive over with the pony and trap and bring home the package—Sparrow, who usually performed these errands, having injured his hand. At my friend's request I was allowed to accompany him, and we set off in high spirits, a number of envious "Foxes" and "Eagles" shouting after us as we passed the playground wall.

Nothing of any importance happened till we reached the Sportsman, where, having fastened up the pony, we went inside to inquire about the parcel. It being the middle of the afternoon the little inn seemed deserted. The only occupant of the taproom was a young country lad, who sat on a big settle, just inside the door, munching a crust of bread and cheese. He turned his head as we entered, and Miles immediately accosted him with,—

"Hullo, Tom Lance! what brings you here?"

The lad was evidently confused at the meeting. His sunburnt face flushed a deeper red, and he mumbled something which we did not hear.

"What brings you in this part of the world?" asked Miles. "Are you tramping it all the way back to Stonebank?"

It had dawned on me by this time who the boy was and where I had seen him before. I remembered now that he was an orphan, and in the employ of Mr. Nicholas Coverthorne. He lived in the house, and made himself generally useful about the farm. Miles had to repeat his question a second time before he got any answer; then the boy, seeming to realize that he could not avoid an explanation sooner or later, blurted out,—

"I'm on the way to Welmington, sir, to go for a soldier."

"To go for a soldier!" cried Miles. "You aren't old enough to enlist."

"I'm big enough, though," replied the boy with a grin; and this seemed likely to prove true, for he was well grown, and might easily have persuaded a recruiting sergeant that he was two years beyond his real age.

"But what are you doing that for?" asked my friend. "Why are you leaving Stonebank?"

Lance hesitated, toying with his huge clasp-knife, and moving uneasily on his seat.

"Well, sir," he said at length, "I've run away. And it's no use your telling Mr. Nicholas or the rest where I'm gone, for I ain't going back, not if they send a wagon and horses to fetch me."

"I'm not going to tell my uncle," was the reply. "All I asked was what made you leave."

"Well, sir," continued the lad, "the master's been so queer of late, I believe he bears ill-will towards me for something, and that some day he'll do me an injury."

By dint of many questions we at length got out of Tom something like a connected account of his troubles. The story as he told it was so disjointed, and at times so incoherent, that I shall make no attempt to repeat it in his own words, but rather give the sum and substance of the narrative which was laid before us when we at length came to the end of our inquiry.

Soon after his brother's death the servants had noticed some change in Mr. Nicholas's manner and behaviour, which they regarded as the effect of his sudden bereavement. He became preoccupied and silent, and of an evening would lock the door of his sitting-room and stay there far into the night, though hitherto he had been very regular in his habits, and had almost invariably retired to bed soon after ten. One afternoon Tom had gone on an errand to Tod's Corner, and being delayed did not return till late. It was nearly eleven when he reached the farm. He saw a light in the parlour as he approached the house, and on entering went at once to inform his master of the result of his mission.

Proceeding to the sitting-room, he found the door standing ajar, and the room unoccupied. The lamp was burning on the table, beside it was a large brass-bound box, and a spirit decanter and glass stood hard by. Tom lingered, note in hand, then determined to leave the message where his master would be sure to see it on his return. To do this he approached the table, but had hardly done so when Mr. Coverthorne burst into the room in a towering rage.

"Who told you to come here?" he shouted, seizing Tom by the throat, as though with the intention of strangling him. "I'll teach you to come prying and meddling about my house when you ought to be in bed, you rascal!"

Nicholas Coverthorne, as any one could have told at a glance, was a powerful man, and the wonder was that in his blind rage he did not do the lad some injury before the latter had time to explain that he had merely stepped inside the room a moment before to deliver his message.

"You've been prying into the drawers and cupboards after tobacco, or anything you could find, that's my opinion," cried his master. "If so, you'd better speak the truth before I find it out for myself."

Tom, equally astonished at this unreasonable outburst, and at the fact of his honesty being called in question—a thing which had never occurred before—was for the time at a loss to find words in which to excuse himself, a fact which seemed to increase all the more his master's suspicions. At length, after a long wrangle and many threats, he was dismissed to bed, whither he gladly betook himself, having by this time arrived at the conclusion that his master had either drunk too much brandy or was losing his reason.

A few days later Mr. Coverthorne sent for the lad, and told him to go to the cottage of the hind and bring back an answer to some inquiry about the sheep.

"If I'm not in the parlour when you return," Mr. Coverthorne had said, "step inside, and wait there till I come back."

In obedience to his orders Tom went to the hind, and returning entered the parlour, only to find that his master was not there. The room presented an exactly similar appearance to what it had done on the occasion of his previous visit: the lamp was lit, and beside it was the brass-bound box, while a little further along was the tray with glass and decanter. Cap in hand, the boy remained standing just inside the door, wondering how long he would have to wait. It was while thus employed that his attention became attracted towards a curtain which covered the bay window at the end of the room. Almost in the centre of the drapery, which was old and faded, was a hole, and behind this something sparkled in the ray of the lamp. It did not take Tom long to discover that this something was an eye peering at him from behind the screen. Startled at the knowledge that he was being watched, the lad was about to run from the room and raise an alarm of robbers, when the curtain was flung aside, and with a laugh Mr. Coverthorne stepped out into the room, and asked the boy in a jocular manner what he was staring at. Nicholas was not given to joking with any man, least of all with his servants, and this erratic behaviour served to strengthen in Tom's mind the impression that his master was certainly going mad.

"Ever since that time I've seen him a-watching, watching me wherever I goes and whatever I does," concluded the boy. "Once he told me what he'd do to any one as couldn't mind their own business, though I'm sure I've not been prying into other folk's affairs. He follows me about; he's got a grudge against me for something—I can see it in his evil eye—and some day he'll pay it off. I won't stay there any longer; I'm going for a soldier."

It was in vain that we tried to dissuade Tom Lance from his purpose, and induce him to return to Stonebank. He stubbornly refused to listen to our arguments. It was evident that he had been some time making up his mind, and was now doggedly determined to carry out his purpose. Finding it impossible to do anything else, we wished him good luck, at the same time giving him a shilling and some loose coppers, which was all the money we had in our pockets.

Having found the doctor's parcel, we returned to the pony carriage, and drove some little distance on our homeward way without speaking. It is probable, however, that the thoughts of both of us were busy with the same subject.

"I wonder if your uncle is going out of his mind," I said at length.

"More likely some deep dodge of his, I fancy," returned Miles. "Don't you see that he arranged that second visit of Tom's to the parlour just to judge what he'd done the time before? If the lad was inquisitive and had pried about once, he'd probably do so again. Still, what's the meaning of it all I've no idea."

CHAPTER VI.

A MAD PRANK.

Time has been called "the great healer;" and as the term ran on Miles gradually regained a measure of his former high spirits, and became more his old bright self again. The thought, however, that at the end of the half he would leave school and we should part, perhaps for ever, hung over us like a cloud, rendered all the heavier and darker by the consciousness on my friend's part that his prospects in life had undergone a great change, and that his future was uncertain.

"It's all very well," he burst out one day, "for Uncle Nicholas to say that he would rather have the matter settled amicably. As I said before, he means to get the whole estate before he's finished."

"Old villain!" I answered; "I hate his very look! I hope, if he does go to Coverthorne, that the ghost will haunt him, and drive him away again. Did it sing any more after I left?"

"I don't know," answered Miles abruptly, as though the subject was one to which he did not care to refer. "I don't think I've been inside the room since we were there together. I suppose I'm a coward, but I don't mind owning that that unearthly row gives me the creeps, and I daresay it would you too if you were to hear it as I have, sometimes, when passing down the passage at night."

We did not pursue the subject any further. Indeed, the thought may have occurred to me that my own courage had ebbed away rather fast the last time I had listened to those strange sounds; and such being the case, I could hardly afford to rally my friend on his superstitious fears.

The days came and went; the trees put on their glorious autumn tints, and then gradually grew bare and lifeless, while we boys went on with our accustomed round of school life, labouring at our desks, and larking with unbounded stock of animal spirits in the playground. I can recollect no event of any particular consequence having happened during this time, except that one day Miles received a letter from home which contained news of interest to us both. In those times, before the introduction of the penny post, letters were less frequent and more highly prized than they are to-day; and I think I can see my friend now as he came down the schoolroom waving above his head the oblong packet sealed with a yellow wafer.

"For me!" he cried. "Hurray! now I shall hear what's been happening in our part of the world."

He flung himself down on the end of a bench, tore open the packet, and for some moments was absorbed in reading its contents. Suddenly I saw the expression of his face change, his mouth opened, and his eye ran more rapidly from line to line.

"Phew! Well, I never!" he exclaimed.

"What is it?" I asked; "anything to do with your uncle Nicholas?"

"No; it's about old Lewis," he answered. Then, after scanning the letter rapidly to the end of the page, he let it fall and raised his head. "I say," he began, "what d'you think's happened? Why, there's been a fight down at Rockymouth between the smugglers and the preventive men; quite a serious affair—two fellows badly injured."

"Was old Lewis one of them—that man whom we saw hiding in your copse, and in whose boat we went fishing?"

"Yes, rather: he seems to have been the leading spirit, and has got into worse trouble than the rest, poor beggar! As far as I can understand from my mother's account, it must have happened in this way. One of the land gang was bribed, and turned informer, so by that means the coastguard knew the exact time and place of the run. It happened in that same little cove where we used to go and bathe. The spirit was landed, and the carriers were just shouldering their tubs to make off inland, when an armed party appeared on the beach and ordered them to surrender. Then there was a pretty how-de-do! Some of the gang threw down their loads and tried to bolt. Most of these got away in the darkness. But the old hands, enraged at the thought of losing the stuff just as it had come into their possession, showed fight. One of the preventive men was knocked down with a bludgeon, the rest drew their cutlasses, and blood was shed on both sides. Lewis, raging like a madman, whipped out a pistol and fired it, though fortunately without doing any harm, and the next moment he was stretched senseless on the shingle with a blow on the head given with the flat of a steel blade. In the end, of course, the coastguard got the best of it. Some of the smugglers made off when they saw the day was going against them, but the rest were overpowered, handcuffed, and dragged off to the watchhouse. Some of them have already been sent to jail, but Lewis has been sent to Welmington to await trial at the assizes. He was recognized as the leader of the party, and as the man who fired the pistol; and to use weapons like that against the king's men is a serious offence. Mother says she thinks he will be transported. It's a crying shame," concluded the speaker, after a moment's pause. "What difference can it make to the king, or to anybody else, if those men buy and sell a few ankers of brandy? They don't injure or rob anybody, and the men who come meddling and interfering with them deserve to be roughly handled. I believe I should have shot at them myself if I'd been in Lewis's place."

Knowing the peculiar views of the coast-bred boy on the subject of defrauding the revenue, and the little likelihood of inducing him to change them, I made no attempt to argue the matter, but stood for a moment recalling to my mind the sight I had witnessed of the two stooping figures crossing the field in the gray twilight of the summer dawn.

"It's dreadful to think of his being transported to the other side of the world," I said. "It must be sad for him to think that he may never see Rockymouth again, where he has lived so long—ever since he was a boy, except the time he spent away as a sailor in the navy."

"Well, it's fortunate that he didn't shoot straighter, or he would have swung for it," remarked Miles bluntly; "though I believe some of those fellows would as soon be hung as transported. I'm glad none of our Coverthorne men appear to have been in it," he added. "It's a wonder they weren't; but perhaps if any of them did lend a hand, they were among those who escaped."

He laughed as though it were more of a prank than a crime; then picking up the sheets of paper which had fallen from his hand, he went on reading his letter.

Boys may remain always much the same in their tastes and dispositions, but, as I have said before, school life and customs have undergone great changes since my day. In consequence of having no properly organized outdoor sports, we found methods of our own for letting off steam, some of which were about as sensible as the antics of a kitten or the mad gallop of a young colt. Boys who wished to establish and keep up a reputation for hardihood and daring were prone to perform some reckless feat, and then dare others to follow their example. Ben Liddle, the acknowledged chief of the "Eagles," was much given to this sort of thing, and a dozen or more of his escapades occur to my mind as I write.

It so happened that this term Miles and I slept in a dormitory of which Liddle was "cock;" an arrangement which might have been unpleasant for us had it not been for the fact that the majority of the boys were "Foxes," and formed a mutual defensive alliance, so that Liddle stopped short of actual violence, knowing that anything of the kind would raise a hornet's nest about his ears. Nevertheless, he was always passing slighting remarks about us, and hinting that we were lacking in pluck and daring; which taunts on one or two occasions nearly brought about a free fight between the rival parties.

The weeks went by; we were close to the end of the half, and boys had commenced to talk of holidays and home, when one night Liddle came up to bed with something under his coat.

"Look here," he said; "I found this in a field this afternoon."

The article which he held up was an ordinary rope halter. He waved it triumphantly in the air, and then flung it into a box by the side of his bed.

"What on earth d'you want with that old thing?" cried one of his followers, laughing; "it's no use to you. What made you bring it home?"

"You know that horse of old Smiley's that he's turned out to graze in that big field—the second beyond the brook? Well, I'm going to make him give me a ride. I've bet Maggers two to one in half-crowns that I'll ride him bareback twice round the field without being thrown."

Seated on the next bed, winding an old turnip-shaped silver watch, was a fellow named Rigby. Though professedly a stanch "Eagle," he seemed lately to have grown rather jealous of Liddle, and to covet for himself the post of leader. Whenever Liddle attempted to impress us with some fresh act of bravado, Rigby either made light of it or tried to outdo it by the recital of some still more brilliant piece of mischief which he had either been guilty of in the past or was prepared to attempt some time in the future. As might be expected, nothing could have been more calculated to vex and provoke Liddle, who, we could see, often found it difficult to restrain himself from vindicating his outraged vanity by pounding with clenched fists the person of his presumptuous follower.

"Pooh!" said Rigby. "When d'you expect you're going to ride a horse round that field? They can see it from the house, and you'd have some one after you within five minutes. I'll bet you'll never try it."

"What'll you bet?" demanded Liddle, bristling up in a moment.

"I won't bet anything on such a stupid thing. I know you won't do it."

"I'll do it any time you like to mention."

"Well, do it now," answered Rigby, suggesting what he considered to be impossible.

"All right; I will," returned Liddle recklessly. "Wait till the lights have been put out and the coast is clear, and I'll go and ride the nag to-night. But look here, my boy," continued the speaker, with a malicious twinkle in his eyes: "if I go you'll have to come too, as a witness, or Maggers won't believe I've won my wager."

"I never said I'd do anything of the kind," answered the other, rather drawing in his horns.

"Ho, ho!" sneered Liddle, perceiving his advantage, and proceeding to make the most of it; "you're funky. You try to make out that other people haven't the spirit to do a thing when really you're afraid to try it yourself."

"I'm not afraid," was the reply; "I only say it can't be done, so what's the good of gabbing about it any further?"

"It *can* be done," asserted Liddle. "All you have to do is to wait till there's no one about, then get out of this window on to the roof of the shed, creep along that, and down by the water-butt, then hop over the wall, and there you are. Come; you've as good as dared me to do it, and I say I'll go and ride the horse if you'll come and see me do it. Now, will you go, or will you not?"

"There's no sense in it," grumbled Rigby.

"Pooh! you mean you haven't got the pluck."

There was a general laugh. Rigby found himself in a trap of his own making. If he drew back he stood a good chance of being exposed to ridicule as an empty boaster, besides practically confessing himself Liddle's inferior in daring. His face twitched with excitement and vexation.

"Oh, very well, I'll go!" he answered desperately. "But I don't see any object in it, all the same."

An hour later, when all was quiet, the two boys, who had only partially undressed, rose, put on the rest of their clothes, and prepared to start.

"Shut the window after us, you fellows," said Liddle, "and be ready to haul us in when we return. We'll chuck a bit of mud or gravel against the glass. Don't get talking or making a row to attract attention; and mind, if any one does come into the room you're all dead asleep."

Arranging a bundle of spare clothes and pillows under their counterpanes as a last precaution, lest the notice of a master entering the room should be attracted by the empty beds, the two boys started on their expedition. The roof of the outbuilding was not far below our window, and with the assistance of a rope made of knotted towels it was reached without much difficulty. There was a whispered "All right!" and we heard the adventurers crawl away in the direction of the water-butt.

Broad awake, and in a state of suppressed excitement, we waited for what seemed hours, now and again speculating in whispers as to what had become of our two comrades, wondering if Liddle would really carry out his intention of riding the horse, and whether they would get back safely without being caught. Once the footsteps of a master passing along the corridor caused us a few moments' suspense; but we lay perfectly still, and the door of the room remained unopened. At length there came an unmistakable rap on the window-pane, the rope was lowered, and Rigby, followed by Liddle, was hauled back into the room.

"I've done it," whispered the latter, undoing the halter, which he had wound round his waist, "I caught the old nag, and had a fine scamper round the field.—Didn't I, Rigby?"

The other affirmed that such was the fact. Both boys were out of breath with running, and flushed with the excitement and success of their enterprise.

The result of the ordeal being to enhance the reputation of both, they now seemed on the best of terms, and appeared to have forgotten entirely the outburst of jealousy which had really occasioned the expedition. For some time we lay awake, listening to a detailed account of the adventure, and it must have been early morning before we stopped talking and fell asleep.

Almost before breakfast next morning a report of what had happened was whispered through the school, in consequence of which Liddle and Rigby became the heroes of the hour. Though nothing more than a piece of senseless bravado, their prank was considered a very fine and spirited exploit; indeed, when compared with the many raids and hunting expeditions of "Eagles" and "Foxes," it was declared that nothing quite so daring had been attempted for a long while.

Such an amount of notice, combined with open admiration, could not be without its effect on the two persons chiefly concerned, and by the time we retired to rest that evening both Liddle and Rigby were puffed up with conceit, and inclined to indulge in any amount of swagger.

"Now then," cried the former, "who's going to ride the old nag to-night? Come; we've given you a lead, and it's simple enough."

"I'm not going," muttered one boy, while the rest sought to evade the challenge with a laugh.

"See here," continued Liddle, in the same boastful manner, "one of you 'Foxes' have a shot. There doesn't seem to be a ha'porth of go among the lot of you!—Now then, Coverthorne, you can ride, so you're the very man. You used to be ready for a lark, but now, for all this half, you seem to have turned into a regular old woman."

Miles's cheek reddened with an angry flush.

"I'm no more a coward than you are yourself," he answered; "but if you choose to do a senseless thing, that's no reason why every one else in the room should follow suit."

"Oh, that's a fine excuse! Why don't you say at once that you're afraid?"

The dialogue was continued in much the same strain, Liddle flinging taunts with ever-increasing bitterness, till I could see that Miles was rapidly losing his temper. At length, perhaps rather weakly, the latter gave way, and declared himself ready to repeat the previous night's performance.

"I'll do it," he said, "if any one will go with me."

Just at the moment, from a boy's point of view, it seemed to me that friendship demanded that I should volunteer to share the risk.

"All right, Miles," I exclaimed. "I'll go with you; it's simple enough."

The other "Foxes" rewarded me with a subdued "Hear, hear!" For their own sakes they were eager enough for us to make the attempt, but I confess that I would gladly have recalled the promise almost as soon as it was made. From the very start, when I found myself crawling along the top of the wall against which the outhouses were built, I heartily wished myself safely back in the dormitory. Still, there was nothing to be gained by anticipating disaster until the worst actually happened, and we both pretended to make light of the whole matter. What such fellows as Liddle and Rigby had done we could certainly accomplish; and, after all, if we had an ordinary amount of luck, the risk was not great.

Miles especially was country bred, and had no difficulty in finding his way in the dark. Not a sound broke the stillness, and no one seemed to be abroad but ourselves. We pressed forward, conversing only in whispers, until in front of us a row of leafless willow trees loomed up out of the darkness.

"This is the brook," murmured Miles. "There's a plank laid across a little further down. Here we are. Now mind how you step."

Gingerly we crossed the frail bridge, not wishing to add a wetting to the other delights of this midnight raid. Two more hedges had to be scrambled through, and we found ourselves in the field in which the old horse had been turned out to graze. Away on some rising ground a little to the right was the farmhouse, and we noticed a light dimly burning in one of the windows.

"I should have thought they'd have all been in bed by this time," said Miles. "Now then," he continued, unwinding the halter, "let's find the nag. Coop, coo-op, coop!"

Whether Blackbird—as we afterwards found the animal's name was—had grown wiser by experience, and was prepared to show objection to having his night's rest disturbed to gratify the idiotic whim of a couple of schoolboys, I can't say, but the fact remains that as soon as we came within twenty yards of him he gave an indignant snort, and went plunging off in the darkness. The thunder of his hoofs on the turf seemed loud enough to be heard up at the farm. I held my breath till all was quiet again; then off we started towards the opposite end of the meadow, Miles attempting to cajole the animal with soothing words and an imaginary capful of corn. Once more Blackbird allowed us, very nearly, to drive him up in a corner; then, with a loud protestation in the shape of a neigh and a snort, he kicked up his heels and went off at a gallop. How long this sort of thing might have lasted, and whether we or the animal would have got the best of it in the end, can never be said; for before the thudding of the hoofs had ceased, a man's form came crashing through the hedge, and an angry voice yelled out,—

"Hey, you rascals! what are you doing with that horse?"

The newcomer was none other than the farmer himself, returning home from a festive gathering at the house of a friend. Passing along the footpath in the neighbouring field, he had heard our voices and Blackbird's stampede, and had come to the conclusion that he was receiving a visit from a couple of horse-thieves.

All this we learned later, but at the moment no other thought entered our minds than to save ourselves by immediate flight. We turned and ran. How we got over the hedges I don't know; I can only remember plunging through them, regardless of scratches and tumbles, as a bather might through a breaking wave. Old Smiley, who had the advantage of knowing the ground better than we did, followed hard at our heels, breathing out threats and curses. If the man had had a gun in his hand, I believe he would certainly have fired.

Suddenly we found ourselves on the bank of the stream. As luck would have it, we happened to have struck it just at the right spot, and Miles's ready wit came to the rescue.

"Quick!" he panted; "over, and draw away the plank, or the beggar will follow us to the school!"

Recklessly we sprang across the narrow bridge; then seizing the plank, with our united strength dragged it over, flung it down on the bank, and rushed off into the darkness.

The ruse proved entirely successful. Though a good runner, old Smiley was not going to attempt a jump with the risk of a ducking. We heard his shouts growing fainter and fainter in the distance, and a few minutes later we had scrambled along the roof of the outhouses, given the signal, and were being hauled up to the window by our comrades, who were on the *qui vive* awaiting our return.

In a few breathless sentences Miles explained what had happened.

"It's all right!" said Liddle reassuringly. "You gave the old beggar the slip finely, and he can never tell that it was two fellows from here. In the darkness he didn't get close enough to recognize your faces."

During the time these few words were being spoken I had been sitting on the end of my bed, endeavouring to regain my breath sufficiently to take part in the conversation. Now raising my hand to take off my cap, I found that it was missing. At once the thought flashed through my mind that I must have dropped it during my flight across the fields, and, what was more, I remembered that my name was clearly marked on the lining. If any of my room-mates had been watching me closely, they must have seen my face lengthen; for should old Smiley or one of his men happen to pick up the cap, it was as good as if they had caught the owner, and my share in the horse-chasing adventure would certainly be discovered.

CHAPTER VII.

TRIED AND SENTENCED.

Every thoughtful person will have remarked how the important events in life are often led up to by some incident or mischance of the most trivial kind; and so this story of mine would, in all probability, never have been written if it had not been for the accidental dropping of my cap in the course of that senseless night adventure.

"Had you got it on when you crossed the brook?" asked Miles, when I explained what had happened. "D'you think you dropped it climbing up to the window?"

In answer to these inquiries I could only shake my head. From the time the farmer surprised us in the field I could only recall a vague impression of our wild scamper through the darkness.

"Oh, it's all right," said Rigby. "I expect it fell off when we were hauling you from the roof of the shed. If so, you can easily get it in the morning."

With that the talk ended, and we scrambled into bed. We had certainly silenced our enemies, and covered ourselves with a questionable kind of glory, by our escapade, for even Liddle admitted that our pluck could no longer be doubted. Yet, as I continued to lie broad awake, staring into the darkness long after my companions had fallen asleep, I was far from easy in mind or satisfied with the result of the adventure.

If I had dropped my cap in the fields and old Smiley found it, he was sure to take it at once to Dr. Bagley and state what had happened. Unfortunately, not more than a month before there had been a passage-at-arms between this same man and us boys, about a broken gate which he declared to have been our doing, though in that instance I think he was mistaken. Still, a formal complaint was made to the headmaster, who addressed us on the subject in the big schoolroom, warning us that in the event of any fresh instances of trespass and damage done by us to neighbouring property being brought under his notice, the culprit would be punished with the utmost severity. All this did not tend to ease my mind as I lay picturing up the possibility of a terrible interview in the doctor's study. There was only one thing I could decide to do, and that was to make search as early as possible on the following day, and try to recover this damaging piece of evidence before it fell into the hands of the enemy. Jumping out of bed next morning at the first sound of the bell, and dressing as hastily as possible, I rushed down into the yard, where, in spite of the cold and darkness, I carefully examined the roof of the outhouses, and the spot by the water-butt where we had climbed up and down. Hunt as I would, however, I was doomed to disappointment—the missing cap was nowhere to be seen; and at length the unwelcome truth was forced upon my mind that it must have fallen off during our flight across the fields, most likely have been dragged from my head as I plunged madly through a hedge.

Standing there shivering in the raw winter morning, I quickly came to the conclusion that I had now no choice but to pursue one course of action. The free time after breakfast was too short to allow of my doing anything till after morning school ended at twelve o'clock; then, even if it meant accepting the risk of being seen, I must run over the ground we had covered the night before, and attempt to find the cap. It was quite possible that neither the farmer nor his men might cross these particular fields before midday, and so, with good luck, this unfortunate proof of my guilt might be kept from falling into their hands.

How vividly the events of that unfortunate morning are impressed upon my mind! We had no separate classroom in those days; the one big school held all the forms in work hours, each division being marshalled round the desk of its particular master. The class which contained Miles

Coverthorne, myself, and about a dozen other boys, was taken by a master named Jennings. We were seated at our desks preparing some work before standing round to be questioned. Exactly what the subject was I don't remember— probably the Latin grammar, to the study of which the greater portion of our time seems to have been devoted. Directly in front of me sat a youth who, from the possession of a peculiarly squeaky voice, was known as the "Jackdaw," a nickname which suited him in more ways than one, for he was as mischievous as the famous bird whom the legend declares to have stolen the cardinal's ring.

My eyes happening to wander from my book, I became aware of the fact that the "Jackdaw" was endeavouring to attract my attention. In the hand which he held out towards me was a queer-shaped object, which he evidently wished me to examine. I took it, and found that it was a toy which he had already informed me he intended to make. The article in question was one which it is probable my present-day readers will never have seen, and I find some difficulty in describing it without being able to demonstrate its working by showing the thing itself. In my young days, when children were more often obliged to make their own playthings, they were common enough. We called them "jumpers," and constructed them out of the breastbone of a goose, a bit of wood, and some twisted string. At the point of the bone was a small piece of cobbler's wax. This was warmed; then the bit of wood was wound round and round in the twisted string, which ran through two holes bored in the extremities of the fork; the end of the chip was then stuck to the wax, and the "jumper" placed ready for its leap. As the wax cooled, its hold gradually relaxed, till suddenly the bit of wood was let go, and, with the action of a compressed spring, sent the whole contrivance flying into the air.

Unable to resist the temptation of seeing how the "Jackdaw's" newly-made treasure would act, I wound up the string, warmed the wax by breathing on it, and foolishly set the toy down on the form by my side. I don't know whether the "jumper" was a specially strong one, but after a few moments' pause it suddenly sprang high in the air, and, describing a circle, fell with a clatter right on the master's desk.

Mr. Jennings looked up with a start from the book he was reading.

"Who did that?" he demanded sharply.

There was a general titter.

"Please, sir, I did," I faltered.

"Then stand out," ordered the master. "If I have to speak to you again for inattention, you will stay in and do your work after school."

As the words were uttered a sudden thought flashed through my mind that if I were kept in after school I should not be able to carry out my intention of slipping off and going in search of my cap. I glanced uneasily towards the end of the room where Dr. Bagley was seated at his desk, giving instruction to the head form. If he happened to catch sight of me thus banished from the class, it might mean further trouble. Fortunately, for the present the great man's attention was fully occupied. I waited anxiously for about ten minutes, and then ventured to ask Mr. Jennings if I might sit down.

"Certainly not," was the reply. "Remain where you are till the end of the lesson."

Hoping that the worst would not happen, I resumed my former position. There was a movement at the end of the room; the doctor had dismissed his boys to their seats to write an exercise. Slowly he rose from his chair, adjusted his spectacles, and, descending from his platform, came down the room. I saw that my fate was sealed, and stood like a condemned criminal on the drop, awaiting the withdrawal of the fatal bolt.

"Well, sir, and what brings you here?"

Not knowing what reply to make, I remained speechless, and Mr. Jennings answered the question.

"He has been wasting his time and disturbing the rest of the class playing with this silly toy, sir."

In those days the cane was the most usual form of punishment for all kinds of offences. Though sharp at the moment, it had the advantage of being soon over; and remembering my project, I almost hoped that the headmaster would order me to follow him to his desk, the usual place of execution. If this, however, was my wish, it was destined to be thwarted.

"Oh, indeed!" returned the doctor, in his most magisterial tones. "Then let me tell you, sir, that a boy who plays in work hours must make up his mind to work in play hours.—Mr. Jennings, kindly set him a task, and see that he remains at his desk during the free hour before dinner."

In my vexation I could have fallen on the "Jackdaw" and given him a good pommelling for having induced me to meddle with such an exceptionally lively "jumper" in school time. The mischief, however, was done now; and when the other boys were dismissed, and rushed out into the playground, I was forced to remain at my place with a Latin book open in front of me, a certain number of lines of which I was ordered to commit to memory.

I was still far from easy in mind, and could only hope that my cap was reposing in some ditch or thicket, where it was not likely to be noticed by any chance passers-by. Attempting to reassure myself with the thought of this possibility, I settled down to my task, and commenced repeating the Latin lines over and over again, in a monotonous undertone, until they should become fixed in my memory.

The hands of the clock must have reached half-past twelve, when the door of the schoolroom suddenly opened, and Sparrow the porter made his appearance.

"Mr. Eden, the doctor wants you—now, at once—in his study;" and with this abrupt announcement the man promptly turned on his heel and disappeared.

To us boys there was always a dreadful significance in that apparently harmless message, and my heart sank within me as I rose to my feet and prepared to obey. I walked down a short, dark passage, across a bare, draughty hall, and knocking on a forbidding-looking door, received a peremptory command to "come in."

Once across the threshold any doubt as to the reason of the summons was set at rest by the sight of Farmer Smiley sitting very bolt upright on a chair by the bookcase, with his hat on the floor by his side.

"D'you see this cap, sir?" began the headmaster, holding up the article in question. "It has your name on the lining, therefore I presume it is yours."

From the burning sensation in my cheeks I felt that my face must have given a plainer answer to the question than my mumbled reply.

"Then will you explain how it came to be lying this morning in the middle of one of Mr. Smiley's fields?"

However unwilling I might be to tell the story, the admissions were dragged from me—first, that I had visited the farmer's field with the object of enjoying a stolen ride on his horse; and, secondly, that I had actually done so late the previous night, when I was supposed to be asleep in bed.

"You actually mean to tell me that you climbed out of your dormitory window and went roaming over the country when it must have been close on midnight? I never heard of such outrageous conduct—never!"

"He warn't the only one," put in the old farmer; "there was two on 'em."

"Was any other boy with you?" demanded Dr. Bagley.

I shut my mouth tightly with the determination that nothing should induce me to betray my friend. Whether the doctor would have insisted on a reply to his question I

71

cannot say, but fortunately a diversion was caused by the farmer, who probably felt satisfied in bringing home the charge against at least one of the culprits.

"Well, whether I seed one or two I ain't perticular about—leastways there's no doubt about this un. And," continued the speaker, going off at a tangent, "it seems to me a pity that a man can't live on a farm without his gates being broken and his beasts chased by a band of mischievous young rascals like this 'ere."

"Mr. Smiley," began the headmaster, "I can only say how much I regret that anything of this sort should have happened. I can assure you that I shall make an example of this boy, and take steps to prevent your meeting with any such annoyances in the future.—Now, sir," he continued, turning to me, "go straight to your bedroom, and stay there till I send for you to come down."

There is no necessity for me to enter into a full description of the painful incidents which followed this command. Dr. Bagley was not in a mood to be lenient. The various raids of "Foxes" and "Eagles" over the countryside had occasioned more than one complaint being lodged against us; and now that he had a clearly-proved case to deal with, the headmaster was determined to make such an example of the culprit as should discourage indulgence in such lawless practices in the future.

That afternoon I received a public caning before the whole school, and was informed that, as an additional punishment, I should be kept back to go home one day later than the rest.

Though the flogging was a severe one, I think I would have endured it a second time if the doctor would have substituted this for the remaining part of my sentence. At the end of a long half every extra day seemed an unbearably long period of time, and the thought of seeing all my comrades start for home while I lingered behind, and missed all the fun of travelling with them—such a prospect, I say, appeared almost unendurable. As has been already stated, owing to the limited accommodation on the coaches, our breaking-up really extended over two days: half the boys were starting on the Wednesday, and the other half on the Thursday; so I should have to remain till the Friday morning. Sitting on the end of my bed in the cold dormitory, where I had been ordered to spend the rest of the day in solitary confinement, I felt the soreness of this disappointment more than the smart of the weals inflicted by the headmaster's cane. There was, however, one consolation through it all—namely, the fact that I had not betrayed my comrade in the night's adventure. However crude our code of honour may have been, we were loyal to it; and I had the satisfaction of feeling that my school-fellows would remember this as a proof that I was no sneak. Furthermore, this was to be the end of Miles's school life, and it would have been a pity for him to finish up by being sent home in disgrace for what was, after all, merely a piece of thoughtless folly, and largely the fault of Liddle.

The short winter day was drawing to a close, and I was sitting in the deepening twilight, when the door suddenly opened, and in came Miles. He had been watching his opportunity to creep upstairs, and was carrying his boots in his hand, it being against the rules for boys to visit the dormitories between the times of getting up and going to bed.

"I say," he began, "I hope I haven't acted like a sneak. I've been thinking that perhaps I ought to have come forward and owned up to having been with you last night, but I'll tell you why I didn't. I thought perhaps the doctor had asked if any one else had gone, and you might have said 'No;' and in that case you'd only have got it worse for not telling the truth. I tried to get to see you before dinner, but I nearly got caught; and though I've been on the lookout ever since, this is really the first opportunity. I say, didn't old

Smiley notice there were two of us? or how did it happen that I escaped?"

I told him exactly what had transpired in the course of my examination by the headmaster.

"You're an awful old brick, Sylvester!" he exclaimed. "It was jolly good of you to try to keep me out of the scrape when it was really my doing. All the same, now I know exactly what you said, I shall go to Bagley and tell him of my share in the business. I can't save you the thrashing, but he might let you off from staying behind that extra day."

"Don't be a fool!" I cried, catching him by the arm. "It can't make any difference now. He won't let me off, and you'll only get in a row yourself. Look here, Miles: you've had trouble enough lately, and I'm only too glad to have kept you out of this row. If you think you're indebted to me for a good turn, then do as I ask, and don't go spoiling it all by getting flogged for nothing."

He laughed, and sat down on the bed by my side.

"You're a regular old brick," he repeated; "and if you really mean it, why, I'll let sleeping dogs lie. But I wish there was more likelihood of my being able to do something for you in return. Who knows if we shall ever meet again? If we are forced to give up Coverthorne, I think I shall go to sea. I must have an open-air life, and I couldn't stand being penned up in an office."

We sat silent for a few moments in the gathering darkness, and I must own to an uncomfortable lump rising in my throat as I strove to find words in which to reply. We had come as new boys to the school on the same day, and had been close friends ever since, sharing our joys and sorrows, and never expecting that a day would come when our companionship would have a sudden and unlooked-for ending. I should have little to look forward to in returning to school after the Christmas holidays.

"Hullo! there goes the tea-bell," exclaimed. Miles. "Cheer up," he added, apparently reading my thoughts; "we shall meet again—who knows?"

"Who knows?" I echoed, as cheerfully as I could, and forcing a laugh.

My friend turned and stole softly from the room. If some one could have told us that we should see each other again before the year was out, we might have spent the night in guessing, and yet have remained without the remotest idea as to how, when, and where that extraordinary meeting was to take place.

CHAPTER VIII.

MY JOURNEY BEGINS.

It was certainly a bitter pill for me to swallow watching the boys start for home on the Wednesday and Thursday mornings, and what made the punishment seem all the harder was saying good-bye to Miles. Had it not been for that hare-brained antic, I might at least have travelled with him on the coach as far as Tod's Corner, and so enjoyed his companionship a few hours longer. A school, after the boys have gone home for the holidays, is a very desolate place. I had my meals at the headmaster's table, but, being in disgrace, ate them in solemn silence, and was glad enough when the ordeal was over, and I was free once more to go where I liked.

At length, on the Thursday afternoon, I found myself sitting at one of the long rows of desks in the empty schoolroom. The unusual quiet seemed to weigh on my spirits; and though I tried to cheer myself with the thought that only a few hours now remained before I should be on the way home, yet a certain gloomy foreboding as of impending trouble seemed to weigh on my mind. What could it be? After all, the loss of one day did not much matter, and I felt sure that when I explained the full circumstances of the case to my parents, they would take a lenient view of my foolish midnight escapade. Sitting idly mending an old quill pen which I had found on the floor, my thoughts turned once more to Miles and his uncertain future, and from this I came to recalling the incidents of my visit to Coverthorne.

What could be the explanation of that strange noise in the so-called haunted room? Of course, there were no such things as ghosts, and yet—and yet I myself had beaten a hasty retreat when left alone with those unearthly sounds, the origin of which it was impossible to trace. The very recollection of the experience made me turn and glance uneasily up and down the long room, as though I half expected to find myself sharing its solitude with some black bogey of a nursemaid's tale. The next instant I laughed at my own foolishness, and rising to my feet began to move about, for the room was cold.

The place had not been swept since the boys' departure. The floor was littered with torn paper, fragments of broken slates, and other rubbish which had been thrown about in the process of packing up. Some light-hearted youth, who had come into possession of a piece of chalk, had covered the blackboard with his scrawlings. Wandering aimlessly up the room, I came to a halt; then, hardly conscious of what I was doing, I opened one of the desks, and glanced down carelessly at its interior.

What good reason I afterwards had to remember that apparently purposeless' action! The books and other boyish possessions had been removed, and nothing remained but a mass of waste paper and other odds and ends, such as lay strewn about on the floor. I stirred this up with my hand. As I did so, my fingers came in contact with something hard, and I drew forth a small, oblong metal box, made, if I remember rightly, of pewter.

The desk had been occupied by a boy named Talbot, who was leaving these holidays, and so had taken his books with him. The object which I held in my hand, and which he had evidently overlooked, was a tinder-box, or rather a box containing tinder, flint, and steel, and little chips of wood tipped with sulphur. The so-called "lucifer" matches, I may remark, did not come into use until some years later. I stood for a moment undecided what to do with my find. Left in the desk it was certain to be discovered and carried off, either by one of the servants or the charwoman who cleaned the room. Talbot had a younger brother who would be returning after Christmas. I might restore the box to him; and with this intention I slipped it into my pocket.

I was up early enough on the following morning, devoured my breakfast in the kitchen by the light of a solitary candle, and then said a hasty good-bye to Dr. Bagley, who had just come down, and who, after sternly expressing a hope that I should amend my ways next term, thawed sufficiently to wish me a merry Christmas and send his compliments to my friends at home. Sparrow was to drive me in the pony-chaise as far as Round Green. We started off, with the single trunk which composed my luggage on the seat in front; and so began the most eventful journey of my life—one which it seems little short of a miracle did not end in my embarking on that still longer journey from which there is no return.

The coach was due to arrive at Round Green at about 9.30, and we were to wait for it, as usual, at the Sportsman Inn, which, being the end of a stage, was always stopped at for the purpose of changing horses.

It was a bitterly cold morning; the roads seemed as hard as iron, and our breath smoked as we talked. We had covered nearly half the distance, and were going along in fine fashion, when suddenly there was a clatter and a crash. I felt myself flung forward, heard a shout from Sparrow, and the next moment found myself rolling down a steep bank by the roadside, half blinded by the cold rime from the frosty grass. It took me a few seconds to recover myself, and when at length I scrambled to my feet, I saw at once what had happened. The pony had slipped on a sheet of ice, and come down badly, cutting its knees and smashing one of the shafts. Fortunately Sparrow had sustained no injury, and with the help of a countryman who happened to be crossing a neighbouring field we unharnessed our steed, and got it once more on its legs.

For a time the accident occupied the whole of our attention. Sparrow was in a fine state of mind, fearing that he would be blamed for the mishap. It was evident that we could not go on, and if we returned we should have to walk.

Then it flashed across my mind that this delay would cause me to lose the coach. There was no catching a later train in those days, and I could not bring myself to face the prospect of spending another day in that deserted school.

"I shall go on," I declared to Sparrow, "and you can return with the pony."

"I doubt if you'll reach the Sportsman in time, Mr. Eden," was the answer. "And there's your box. We must back the chaise into the roadside till it can be sent for, but we ought not to leave your box."

"Oh, bother my luggage!" I began, when the countryman interrupted and came to the rescue.

"I doan't mind carrying the young gen'leman's box as fur as the Sportsman for a mug o' beer," he remarked; "then you can get back home with the pony."

The arrangement was no sooner suggested than I agreed to it, and Sparrow was obliged to acquiesce. The damaged carriage was pushed back into a gateway, my trunk was lifted out, and hoisted on to the broad shoulders of the labourer; and taking leave of the school porter, I turned to resume my journey to Round Green.

In the heat of the moment I had not paid much attention to the doubt expressed by Sparrow as to my reaching the inn in time to catch the coach, but now I began to wonder myself whether the thing could be done. Nowadays every boy has a watch; then they were a rarer possession. I had no means of telling the time, but guessed we had none to spare.

On I went, the man with the box trudging behind me. It soon became evident that, burdened as he was, he could not keep up with me unless I moderated my pace; and at length, when we reached the top of a rather stiff hill, he was obliged to stop and put down the trunk, in order to rest and regain his breath.

The sunshine sparkled on the frosted trees and hedges. It was one of those clear, still winter mornings when sounds carry a long distance, and as we waited there came to our ears the far-off "toot-toot" of a horn. It was the coach signalling its approach to Round Green. I sprang to my feet, and abandoning my box to its fate, rushed off along the road, with some wild notion of stopping the coach and leaving word for my luggage to be sent on. But I might as well have attempted to overtake the vehicle which had carried off my companions on the previous day. The inn was still more than a mile distant, and when at length, flushed and panting, I arrived in front of the building, the only trace to be seen of the *Regulator* was a glimpse of the steaming horses, which had worked the last stage, being led away by an hostler in the direction of the stables. Accustomed though I was to take hard knocks at school, I must say that I could have sat down and cried with vexation. Pulling myself together, I walked into the house, and there encountering Peter Judson, the landlord, and his wife, a stout, good-natured body, who always took a kindly interest in us boys, in a few words I related exactly what had happened.

"What stuff and nonsense not allowing him to go home with the rest!" exclaimed Mrs. Judson. "It just serves that old Dr. Bagley right, his chaise being broken!—Well, my dear," she continued, "I don't see there's anything to be done but for you to go back, and make a fresh start again to-morrow. The butcher will pass in about an hour's time; he is going Ashbridge way, and would take you along with him in his cart."

"Oh, I'm not going back," I answered doggedly. "Look here," I added, struck with a sudden idea: "I'll wait here, and go on by the night coach. I don't mind the cold, and I should get home to Castlefield in time for breakfast to-morrow morning."

"It's not certain you'd find room," muttered Peter, "unless you booked a place beforehand. There's a good many travelling now, just before Christmas."

"Oh, they'd stow him away somewhere, a little chap like him," remarked Mrs. Judson.

Just then a man's head appeared at the door of the bar-parlour in which we were talking, and I recognized Bob, the head stableman, who had been passing down the passage and had overheard our conversation.

"There's the *True Blue* put on extra to-day for the jail delivery," he remarked. "The young gen'leman might get through to Castlefield all right on that. I don't suppose he'd have any particular objection to going along of the 'birds,' seeing they're well looked after!"

The exact meaning of this speech I did not comprehend, but I gathered from it that there was a chance of my going on by an extra coach, which would pass before the mail, and I at once jumped at the opportunity.

"Oh yes; I'll go on by that," I exclaimed. "What time is it due?"

"About half-past four," answered the man.

Judson and his wife looked at each other and then at me.

"I don't see why he shouldn't go," remarked the latter. "George'll look after him all right. Besides, his friends will be expecting him to-day, and'll be sure to be sitting up. He ought to be home just afore or after midnight."

It was, accordingly, settled that I was to go on by the *True Blue*, which was due to pass at half-past four. The man appeared shortly after with my box. I gave him his mug of beer, and then settled down to while away the time as best I could till the coach should arrive. I looked over some back numbers of the *Welmington Advertiser*, went outside and chatted with the stablemen, and joined the landlord and his wife at their midday dinner. Slowly the afternoon wore away. Mrs. Judson had forced me to eat a hearty tea—"to keep out the cold," as the good soul put it—and I was standing warming myself by the taproom fire talking to Judson, when, happening to turn my head, I saw a man's face pressed close against the outside of the window. By this time it was quite dark. I could see nothing more of the stranger than his face, but from the way in which he moved his head it seemed to me that he was endeavouring to get a glimpse of the old eight-day clock which stood in a corner of the room behind the bar. Perceiving that I was looking at something, the landlord turned also, but had hardly done so when the face disappeared.

We waited for a moment, expecting that the stranger would enter the inn; then, as he did not appear, Judson strolled outside to see what the man wanted. I waited some time, and at length the landlord returned.

"You saw that fellow outside, didn't you, sir?" he asked. "Well, it's curious I can't see no trace of him anywhere. He looked rather a rough customer. I wonder what he wanted."

We had little time for speculation, for hardly had my companion finished speaking when the cheerful note of the horn gave warning that the coach was approaching; and the quiet little inn woke up at once with an unwonted show of life and bustle.

Great was my delight, as the guard of the coach entered the room, to recognize our old friend George Woodley, who, I afterwards discovered, had been changed from the *Regulator* to the *True Blue*; and in a few words I explained to him the situation in which I was placed.

"Oh, very well, sir," he answered, "come along; there's a seat outside, and we'll look after you all right."

I followed him down the passage and outside, where the fresh horses were just being put to—the glaring lamps of the coach sending forth rays of light into the darkness ahead, which seemed to make it all the more intense, though stars twinkled overhead. As we stepped into the road we were greeted with a roar of men's voices singing, without much regard to tune or time. The sound came from the outside passengers, who seemed to be diverting themselves with a sort of rough taproom chorus. I remember noticing that the usual pile of luggage on the roof was missing, and to my surprise the box-seat by the side of the coachman was vacant. Into this lofty perch it was that I now climbed; and as the driver gathered up his reins, on the point of starting, an incident happened which caught my attention. A man emerged from the deep shadow of the hedge at the roadside, and springing lightly on to the near front wheel, said in a hoarse whisper,—

"Is that you, Ned? Good-bye, old man! Here, shake hands. Good-bye—God bless you!"

There followed a sharp metallic jingle, which caused me to turn my head; and then it was that, for the first time, I became aware of the fact that the men behind me were all fettered.

CHAPTER IX.

THE RISING.

Tom Barker, the coachman, had just given the word to the hostler to "let 'em go!" when Judson came running out of the lighted doorway of the inn with something in his hand.

"Here's a hare and a brace of pheasants the squire wants delivered to Dr. Plumer of Castlefield, Tom," he said. "They may as well go on by you. I'll hang 'em on the lamp iron."

"All right," muttered Barker, and off we went. To sit beside the driver was in those days considered a very privileged position, and I felt not a little proud of the honour, in spite of the fact that I was filled with a feeling of uneasiness and astonishment at what I had just discovered with regard to my fellow-travellers. The good-natured driver must have guessed my thoughts, for he turned to me, remarking,—

"I suppose you know what sort of a load we've got to-night, sir?"

"Well, no—not exactly," I replied.

"Why, it's the jail delivery off to Botany Bay," was the answer.

"And what's the 'jail delivery'?" I asked, remembering that I had heard the words before, but still in doubt as to their exact meaning.

"Why, these is all jail-birds off to a warmer climate like the swallers," answered Tom, chuckling at his own grim joke, and skilfully winding up the long lash of his whip. "They've all been condemned to transportation at Welmington Assizes, and now they're on their way from jail to the hulks at Portsmouth."

Any doubt as to the correctness of this statement was dispelled by the convicts themselves, who launched out once more into their uproarious song, "We're off to Botany Bay," accompanying their chant with a weird jingling of their chains. This last sound sent a momentary thrill of horror through me, for I had never before seen human beings chained like brute beasts.

"They're all right!" continued Tom. "They've got the ruffles on, and they're all fast to the rail," he added, referring to an iron rail which ran across the coach behind the seat on the roof, to keep the luggage from slipping forward. "They can't do no harm. All the same, I've carried loads I liked better."

"How many are there?" I inquired.

"Ten, and two warders—one inside, and t'other out. There's one they've got inside, a regular highflier—Rodwood his name is. He's sentenced for life, I believe. The only wonder is he's escaped being hung."

"What was his crime?"

"Forgery—at least that's what they've got him for; but they say he's a desperate villain—one as'll stop at nothing when his blood is up, and would think no more of killing a man as came in his way than you or I might of knocking down a rat in a stable. Well, he's off safe enough now for t'other side of the world, and I hope they'll keep him there."

The convicts continued to sing and shout, then grew quieter, apparently tired by their exertions, though every now and again one or more of them burst out afresh in a forced manner, as though bent on making a display of bravado and unconcern. Once or twice, in the pauses of their singing, and amid the clatter of the horses' hoofs and the rumble of the wheels, I remember catching a slight sound, the origin of which it was impossible for even my sharp ears to clearly distinguish, but which I attributed to the swaying and grating of the lamp-iron on which the game had been hung.

On and on we rattled through the darkness. Tom and I exhausted our topics of conversation, and for the time being relapsed into silence. Guilty as I knew my fellow-passengers were of serious crimes, I could not help in a way feeling sorry for them, and contrasting their journey with mine—I myself on the way to the enjoyment of a jolly Christmas holiday with friends at home, and they to banishment from their native land, and to hard servitude beyond the sea.

The cold, too, was intense. I felt it, though warmly clad, and made sure that the poor wretches on the seats behind must be chilled to the bone. Even burly Tom Barker, protected with a driving coat and a big shawl, growled out that "it was a sharp un to-night, and no mistake," by which I understood him to imply that it was freezing hard.

At length, at the end of a stage, as we drew up outside an inn very similar to the Sportsman, Tom prepared to dismount from his perch, and invited me to do the same. I preferred, however, to remain where I was, and was watching the stablemen removing the horses, when, to my surprise, I heard a man's voice behind me pronounce my name.

"Mr. Eden."

Turning sharply, I found the convict directly behind me leaning forward in his seat. The bright light which shone out through the open door of the inn fell directly on his face, and I was shocked to recognize the rugged features of the man Lewis, in whose boat at Rockymouth, on more than one occasion, Miles and I had gone fishing.

"Excuse me, sir," continued the man. "I knew you as soon as you got up at Round Green. Maybe you've heard from Mr. Miles how I come to this. A tussle with the preventive men was what done it. I'm no thief."

Had it not been for the sadness of the situation, I could almost have smiled at this fresh proof of the dogged conviction, entertained by this man and his class, that defrauding the revenue was no crime.

"I should like to have said good-bye to Mr. Miles," continued Lewis. "Give him my respects when you see him. I suppose, sir, you haven't got such a thing as a bit of baccy about you?"

Remembering our holiday excursions, and somehow contrasting his present hapless condition with the freedom of the great sea, I could not but pity the unhappy fellow. I shook my head, signifying that I had not.

The next moment Tom Barker emerged from the inn, rubbing his mouth with the back of his hand. He clambered into his place; there was a "Give 'em their heads, Dick," and we were off again.

The next stage was not accomplished quite so successfully as the previous part of the journey. After a time one of the wheelers went lame. On examination, it proved to have been badly shod, and at the end of another mile Tom pulled up at a wayside blacksmith's to have the offending nail extracted. Here we had to wait some little time while the smith, who had stopped work for the day, was fetched from his cottage, which was down a dark lane, and not easy to find. It was during this pause in the journey, after the coach had remained stationary for about twenty minutes, that a man thrust his head out of the window and demanded, in loud and peremptory tones, the reason of the delay.

"See here, guard," he cried, "this sort of thing won't do! I'm due aboard one of the king's ships to-morrow!"

The convicts sent up a shout of laughter at this reference to the hulk for which they were bound, and I was soon aware that the speaker was not the warder, as I had at first imagined, but the man Rodwood of whom Tom had spoken. He kept up the joke with a few more sentences of a similar kind, until the gruff command, "Stow that!" from the warder caused him to subside once more into his seat. He spoke like an educated gentleman, and with the air of one accustomed to command. Indeed, I afterwards learned that he had once held a commission in the army, but owing to gambling debts had been obliged to sell out, whereupon he had entered upon a career of crime, which had terminated in a sentence of transportation for life. At length George Woodley and the smith put in their appearance; the injured horse was attended to, and we were enabled to resume our journey. Bowling along mile after mile in the darkness, it was difficult to judge how time was passing; but Tom, glancing at his old, turnip-shaped watch as we left the smithy, muttered,—

"Blessed if it ain't quarter-past eight, and we ain't got to Tod's Corner."

The mention of the crossroads, where at the beginning of the summer holidays we had been met by the gig from Coverthorne, caused my thoughts to fly off to the old house and the fun I had had with Miles, both at the commencement of the previous holidays and during that long friendship which had been brought to such an untimely end. Musing over the events of the holiday naturally led me back to a remembrance of the man with whom I had just been speaking. There he sat, bound for the opposite side of the globe; yet within half an hour we should pass within three miles of Rockymouth, that native village which he might never behold again. If it had been daylight, we should by this time have caught a glimpse of the sea from the highway along which we were travelling, and the night air seemed flavoured with the salt odour of the ocean.

Though cold and weary, the convicts had once more commenced their song, as though, being debarred the free use of their limbs, they were determined to keep themselves warm with the exercise of their lungs. I had grown by this time so much accustomed to their presence as to hardly notice their shouting; tired out with the day's adventures, only the fear of falling from my lofty perch prevented my dropping off to sleep. Even the sharp tingling of my ears would not have kept me awake. My chin kept falling with a jerk upon my breast, and the clatter of hoofs and the song of the prisoners mingled strangely with momentary fancies that I was back at school, or was talking with the loved ones at home.

At length I was roused up broad awake by the coach stopping. The road was very dark, owing to its being overshadowed by a number of tall trees. I peered about me, and catching sight of a ruined cottage with half of its thatched roof fallen in, I recognized the spot at once, and knew that we were come to within about a mile of Tod's Corner. Just beyond the glare of our lamps was the brow of a steep and dangerous hill, and we had pulled up while George jumped down and put on the drag.

In fancy I can see now the dark figure of Tom Barker beside me, reins in one hand and whip in the other, waiting for the signal to proceed. The convicts had ceased their singing, and all was quiet except for the impatient scrape of one of the leader's hoofs. I heard the tinkle of the drag as Woodley loosed the chain; then on the roof behind some one gave a short, sharp whistle.

Exactly what happened next I did not fully realize till later. Two men suddenly seized Tom Barker from behind, and a desperate struggle ensued. The silence was broken by an outburst of horrible threats and cursing, while, to make matters worse, the horses, startled by the noise and the fall of the coachman's whip on the backs of the wheelers, sprang forward, and, as though knowing instinctively that something was wrong, gave every sign of commencing to bolt.

I fear I cannot claim for myself any particular presence of mind: it was more the natural impulse of self-preservation which prompted me to act; for once let the horses start to gallop down that hill, and all our necks were as good as broken. Fortunately, although I had never enjoyed the privilege of handling the ribbons on a stage-coach before, I was accustomed to horses. I seized the reins in the nick of time, just as they were slipping over the splashboard, and bracing myself for the effort, succeeded in bringing the team to a standstill.

Even as I did so Tom Barker was flung from his seat, and fell heavily into the road, where he lay like a log, stunned if not dead. Terrified by this violence, I was about to spring down and make good my escape in the darkness, when I felt my arm seized in an iron grip, and a voice, which I recognized as belonging to the man Lewis, spoke in my ear.

"Stay still, sir; you may get hurt if you try to run. I'll see you come to no harm."

CHAPTER X.

HIGHWAY PIRATES.

It did not take me long to arrive at an understanding of the true state of affairs. The convicts had risen, overpowered their guards, and seized the coach. From scraps of conversation which passed between them, I subsequently learned that the man whom I had seen appear and disappear so mysteriously outside the Sportsman Inn was a friend of one of the prisoners, and, under the pretence of wishing him good-bye, had handed up a couple of small files, with which several of the men had freed themselves from their fetters. Once or twice I had heard a slight grating noise, but, as I have already said, I had attributed the sound to the swaying of the lamp.

By some method of communication such as criminals seem always able to establish, the three convicts inside had been informed of what was about to take place, so that at the same moment the outbreak took place on the roof they flung themselves on the warder who rode with them, and succeeded in holding him down and wresting from him the pistol with which he was armed.

To a certain extent stupefied by the shock of this sudden surprise, I had but a confused notion of what took place during the next ten minutes. Together with George Woodley, who had also been seized, I was thrust to the side of the road, while a man told off to keep watch over us ordered us gruffly to sit down facing the hedge with our feet in the ditch, as a greater precaution against our making any sudden attempt to bolt.

In this position we could only judge by the sounds and conversation going on behind us what was actually taking place.

"Better keep still, Master Eden," whispered George. "We'd be safer in a cage of wild beasts than among these men at this moment."

Obtaining the keys of the handcuffs from the pockets of their guards, those men who had not already freed themselves from their fetters were speedily liberated; the warders were now gagged, chained, and, as a further precaution, bound with the broad straps used for securing luggage on the coach roof. Not till this had been done was any heed paid to poor Tom Barker, who lay in the road exactly where he had fallen.

"Is he dead?" I heard a voice inquire callously.

"Can't say," was the gruff reply. "There's blood from his head on the stones. Hand down that lamp, and let's have a look. He's breathing," continued the speaker after a pause. "I should say he'll come round again before long."

At that moment a man, whom I recognized at once as Rodwood, bade every one be silent and listen to what he had to say. The hum of voices ceased, and the men gathered round the speaker, who raised himself by standing on one of the steps of the vehicle.

"Whatever happens now, there's no turning back," he began; "and what's to be done must be done quickly. The mail to Welmington will pass before long; and what's more, they'll be expecting us at the end of this stage, so after a while they'll send a man back to find out what's happened. For the present we're all in the same boat, and we'd better all pull together. The thing will be to choose a leader. Now, who'll you have?"

"Yourself," cried a voice, and to this there was a unanimous murmur of approbation.

"Very well," exclaimed the newly-appointed captain, jumping down into the centre of his gang. "Then the first thing is to get these two 'screws' out of the road. They'd have shot us if they could have got at their barkers, and I propose to serve 'em the same way. It's the safest plan. Hand me the pistols!"

The awful coolness with which the man made this terrible proposal thrilled me with horror. Left to himself, the fellow would, I feel sure, have carried out his abominable intention; but his comrades, hardened and reckless offenders as some of them were, could not be persuaded to follow him to such extremes of crime.

"No, no, Rodwood," cried one and another; "there's no need to risk being scragged. Hoist them inside this empty cottage; that'll give us a fair start before they're likely to be found. Put the coachman in there too, and tie his legs; he won't find voice enough to shout for help for some time yet, even if any one chanced to hear him."

The warders and poor Tom were accordingly half lifted, half dragged inside the ruined cottage, and the men came back to decide what was to be done next.

"Where are we going?" asked several voices.

"Well, we must clear out from here," answered Rodwood. "The whole countryside will be raised up against us before morning. We've got a coach and horses at our disposal, so why not go off in that? I'll drive, if no other man wants to handle the ribbons."

"That's all very well," muttered a man named Ned Arch, the convict to whom the file had been given. "That's all very well, but we can't go farther than the end of this stage. They'll be on the lookout there to change the horses, and they'll see at once that something's wrong if we try to drive through without stopping."

"True," answered Rodwood. "We must get off the main road."

It was at this point that I heard Lewis suddenly break in on the conversation.

"If there's no better plan going," he said, "why not make for the coast? We ain't above four miles from Rockymouth, I reckon, and once there I'll undertake to hide you all in a place where you can lie for a time with no danger of being found. I've got friends there to whom, with a bit of care, we can apply for help; and with anything like luck we ought to be safe across the water, every one of us, by this day week."

"Bravo!" cried Rodwood. "Trust a bold 'free trader' for finding a way out of a tight corner. There's our plan of campaign all ready made."

"Look here," broke in the man who had been standing guard over myself and George Woodley. "What's to be done with this pair, I'd like to know? You don't mean to leave 'em sitting here, I suppose?"

"I'd forgotten about the guard and that boy," exclaimed Rodwood. "Take them across the field, and tie them each to a tree in the copse yonder; but gag them first."

Fortunately for us, this suggestion on the part of their leader did not meet with the approval of the other convicts.

"Don't be hard on the lad," said one. "If he hadn't pulled up the horses, we should most of us have had our necks broken."

"Woodley's a good fellow too," remarked another: "he gave us all the baccy he had on him. Tied to a tree, that youngster will be dead of cold before morning; as for the 'screws,' why, they must take their chance."

"Well, these must take their chance too," returned Rodwood angrily. "If they come to be mixed up in this business, that's their own lookout, and not our fault."

"The boy will be frozen on a night like this," said a voice. "He did us a good turn, so why not take him with us? We shall find a chance of dropping him, and the guard too, later on."

"Take him with us!" retorted the leader. "We shall have enough trouble to get off as it is, without dragging a couple of informers round the country with us."

A heated discussion followed. Strange and out of place as it seemed in the breasts of such rascals, a sense of gratitude for what I had done, and for sundry little tokens of commiseration on the part of the kind-hearted George, mingled with their delight at finding themselves so far on the road to freedom, prompted them to show some return in preserving us from injury. It was freezing hard, and the cold was likely to increase still more before morning; therefore it was more than likely that a boy like myself, already tired out with the journey and the long day's adventures, if tied to a tree without the chance of moving about to keep up the circulation, would ultimately perish from the effects of the exposure, if he did not actually die before he was discovered. For the warders there was certainly more hope: the walls of the cottage afforded them a certain amount of shelter from the cutting wind, and, as I afterwards discovered, they had been flung down on some straw, which added to the warmth of their clothing. Rodwood might have ordered us to be put in the same place, but he feared that, if too many prisoners were huddled together in such a confined space, they might roll together on the floor, and in some way contrive to loosen each other's bonds.

It need hardly be said that I listened with straining ears and beating heart as the discussion proceeded. From Woodley's attitude I could tell that he, too, was on the alert; and but for the fact that our captors were now in possession of firearms, I think he might have attempted to spring to his feet and break away from the group with a sudden rush. At length Lewis turned the balance in our favour by declaring that unless we were allowed to accompany the party he would not act as guide, at the same time promising to hold himself responsible for our safe custody until the gang should have effected their escape.

Rodwood perhaps knew that his authority over the party was, after all, of a very nominal kind; and fearing to risk a mutiny before he should have made his position as captain still more assured, he at length gave in, merely insisting that we should be secured in some way to prevent the possibility of our escape.

"Once they get free we're as good as lagged again.—But," he added menacingly, turning in our direction, "you'd better try no tricks on with me, d'ye hear? There's no turning back as far as I'm concerned. It's life or death for me, and I'll make it a life-or-death matter for any one who tries to come between me and liberty."

Without further discussion Woodley and I were, accordingly, ordered to take our places inside the coach, where, to make doubly certain of our safekeeping, we were handcuffed together. It was no good expostulating; we could only submit, and feel thankful at receiving no worse treatment at the hands of these desperate men. But the grip of that cold steel on my wrist made me realize, more than anything else had done hitherto, the perilous nature of our situation. There was no knowing how long the friendly attitude on the part of the convicts would last, or what would be our fate if they were pursued, or were hard pressed in their attempt to escape.

Precious as every moment was to them, they still delayed making a start. One fellow, in whom the plundering instinct seemed to rise even stronger than that of personal safety, had opened the hind boot, and discovered, stowed away there, a large Christmas hamper which, among other things, contained two bottles of wine. Breaking the neck of one of these, and using a metal cup belonging to a flask found in the pocket of the coachman, the men drank all round, pledging each other with rough jests and hoarse laughter. Rodwood alone chafed at this waste of time, but once more found his authority of too brief duration to enforce obedience to his wishes. The men would probably have insisted on discussing the contents of the second bottle, had not something happened which drove even the thoughts of liquor from their minds. Clear and distinct on the frosty air came the clatter of horses' hoofs, and at the same moment the man who had been standing at the heads of our leaders called back the unwelcome news that a coach was coming from the direction of Tod's Corner.

It was then that, for the first time, Rodwood really asserted himself, and proved his natural capacity as a leader. Among his followers the sudden alarm created something like a panic; left to themselves they would certainly have abandoned the *True Blue* where it stood, and made off over the neighbouring hedges and fields—a proceeding the fatal consequences of which, as far as their own interests were concerned, it was not difficult to realize. With curses, and even with blows, Rodwood dashed here and there, seizing the men who were already turning to fly, and forcing them to take their places on the coach.

"As for you two," he said hurriedly, poking his head through the coach window, "if you value your lives, keep your mouths shut.—You understand, Nat?" turning to the man who rode inside to act as our guard.

"Yes, I understand," muttered this ruffian grimly. "They won't have the chance to say much, I'll warrant!"

The speaker was one of the least friendly disposed towards us of the whole gang. He had armed himself with a big stone, and sitting directly opposite Woodley and myself, would certainly have brained one or the other of us if we had made the faintest attempt to give an alarm.

In another moment there was a jerk as the vehicle started and went slowly grinding down the steep hill. About half-way we met the other coach coming up, and for one moment, as the glare of the lamps shone full upon us, I held my breath, wondering whether the escape would be discovered. The man Nat raised his stone in a threatening manner, but neither George nor I had any intention of risking a smashed skull by an outcry which would probably be lost amid the clatter of hoofs and the noise of the wheels.

The tension lasted only a few seconds. Rodwood, who had picked up and put on poor Tom's characteristic beaver hat, played his part well, returning the gruff salutation of the driver of the mail with the greatest coolness. We slipped by into the darkness, and the crisis was past.

So, handcuffed to Woodley, the captive of a gang of highway pirates, I entered on the third stage of that eventful holiday journey.

CHAPTER XI.

THE LAST OF THE "TRUE BLUE."

Under the guidance of Lewis, who acted as pilot, we must have turned down a lane before reaching Tod's Corner, and on leaving the main road our two large lamps were promptly extinguished. The wonder was that the cumbrous vehicle was not overturned twenty times in the first mile. Any ordinary driver might have refused to make the attempt in broad daylight, and on a dark night it needed skill as well as courage, both of which, however, Rodwood seemed to possess in a marked degree. I heard afterwards that in his palmy days he had owned and driven a coach of his own, which no doubt accounted for the masterly way in which he handled the ribbons.

The hour would now have been considered late by country people. There was little chance of any one being about; the chief risk, and that a remote one, lay in the possibility of encountering and being challenged by a "riding officer," a branch of the preventive service whose duty it was during the night to patrol and examine lanes and byroads near the coast, and thus hamper the movements of the smugglers on shore. Though I did not know it till later, this chance of being stopped had been discussed by Lewis and the leader of the gang, who, in the event of such a thing taking place, was fully prepared to resort to desperate measures, and drove with a pistol ready cocked lying on the seat by his side.

On and on we went, jolting and lurching like a fishing-smack in a choppy sea. There was no singing now; the men, as might have been expected, were watchful, and intent on making good their escape. The coach's disappearance from the highroad might not be discovered for some hours yet; on the other hand, any belated farm-labourer, hearing or seeing us as we lumbered past in the darkness, would surely guess that something unusual was happening, and might raise an alarm.

It is difficult for me to recall my own personal feelings at this stage of the adventure. I think I had too much confidence in the good will shown by Lewis and the other men whom we had in a small way befriended to feel really afraid. I was chiefly curious to know where the hiding-place existed in which we should be so securely stowed. Perhaps it was some secret loft or cellar, many of which Miles had declared existed at Rockymouth. Here we should no doubt lie till the following evening, when the convicts would continue their escape by land or water, and George Woodley and I would be set free.

How long we continued jogging onward at a walking pace I cannot say; we should certainly have been overturned had we attempted to go faster, and even at that slow rate it seemed to me that we must have gone miles beyond our destination, and possibly have travelled far along some byroad running parallel with the coast. Then suddenly the coach stopped; there was a murmur of conversation, and we heard the men clambering down from the roof.

A moment later the door was opened, and a voice ordered us to dismount—a feat which it was not altogether easy for Woodley and me to accomplish, still fettered as we were, wrist to wrist. The moment I was outside the vehicle the fresh salt breath of the sea saluted my cheeks and nostrils. We stood on the high ground above Rockymouth, and the narrow lane along which we had come now emerged from between high hedges and cultivated ground, and crossed a stretch of open common or moorland. A mile distant, and far beneath us, the little haven snuggled down in the sheltering valley, the only sign of its existence being one tiny point of light from some cottage window where perhaps watchers sat beside a sickbed.

The last of the outside passengers was helped down from the roof as though he had suffered some injury and was partially disabled. I could not see clearly enough to distinguish what was really the matter with him, but I noticed that in all his subsequent movements he seemed to be led or supported by one of his companions.

By mutual consent the men gathered round us in a group, while the tired horses shook their heads and champed their bits. There we stood, a strange company, and in the silence, broken only by their heavy breathing, a feeling of apprehension began to take hold of me, and I wondered what would happen next.

"What's the time?" demanded Rodwood abruptly. "The guard's got a watch; just have a look, some of you."

The "flink" of a flint and steel was sufficient to show the position of the hands on the broad face of the old-fashioned timepiece, and a voice murmured, "Close on ten."

"Well, boys," began Rodwood, "the first question is, What's to be done with the coach? We can't go to sea in her; and if we leave her here, it's as good as giving the whole countryside information as to our whereabouts."

For a moment there was a silence. A coach and four is not a thing that can be hidden away in the nearest hedgerow, and hitherto the convicts had regarded it merely as a means of escape. At length the man named Nat, who had ridden inside as our guard, spoke up. He had struck me all along as a reckless rascal, and his suggestion certainly confirmed the opinion I had formed.

"Why not send her over the cliffs?" he asked. "No chance of her being found then. I know this coast—a sheer drop into the water in most places. The horses can be turned loose on the common, and I don't suppose they'll be noticed for a day or so. Even when they are found, no one can say very well where they come from."

This outrageous proposal seemed to appeal to the leader of the gang.

"Bravo!" he exclaimed. "Come on, my lads! Where's the 'free trader'? He'll show the way."

The idea of the old *True Blue* being wantonly hurled over the cliffs into the sea was too much for poor George Woodley. He burst out into a torrent of angry expostulations, but was promptly silenced by Rodwood, who flourished a pistol in his face, at the same time bidding him hold his tongue unless he wished to follow the coach on its last journey.

With Lewis and Rodwood in front, two men leading the horses, and the rest of the party, George and myself included, following behind in a sort of funeral procession, we went stumbling across the common. Once I thought I heard Lewis expressing some dislike to the business in hand, but his objections, if such they were, were speedily overridden. Rodwood was beginning to feel his feet more as leader of the party, and enforced obedience to his commands with a swagger and bluster which was well calculated to win respect from his jail-bird following. The murmur of the sea grew more and more distinct as we neared the dark line of headlands; then, at length, the swaying coach came to a standstill.

"Now, then, get their clothes off them!" ordered Rodwood.

The command had reference to the horses, from which the harness was speedily stripped and flung inside the coach. With a cut of the whip they were then driven off into the darkness. As the common extended some distance down the coast, it was probable that before daylight the animals would have strayed far from the spot where they had been liberated.

"Save the lamps," was the next command, "and see if there's anything in the fore or hind boot."

Owing to the peculiar character of its passengers, the coach was found to be carrying practically nothing in the way of luggage, except my own trunk and the one large hamper already mentioned, which had been pushed into the boot for conveyance to Castlefield, probably to relieve the mail, which was sure to be heavily laden at this time of the year. From the gruff remarks of the would-be plunderers, it was evident that they were disappointed. It was probably within the knowledge of most of them that a stage coach sometimes carried a valuable cargo; in fact, not more than two years after the date of my story a bank parcel containing notes and gold to the value of £5,700 was stolen from a coach running between Glasgow and Edinburgh—the thieves in this instance travelling as inside passengers, and cutting a hole with brace-bit and saw through the body of the coach into the boot, from which the plunder was then extracted.

However, a basket of provisions was, in a way, a valuable find; for the question of food was likely to become a serious problem before the members of the gang regained their full freedom. Rodwood therefore told off two of his followers to carry the basket, refused to allow the men to drink the other bottle of wine, and bade one of the party unhang the game from the lamp-iron and carry it slung over his shoulder.

My box was forced open and speedily overhauled; but as it contained little besides spare clothing, it was flung back into the coach. It would have been useless for me to expostulate and claim my property—the rascals were not likely to leave such a piece of evidence lying about on the grass—and I held my tongue.

"It's half-tide," I heard Lewis mutter. "There's a ledge of rock she'll land on, but the flood will carry off the wreckage."

The last moments of the *True Blue* had come.

"Turn her round and back her over," ordered Rodwood.

Awed by the thought of such wanton destruction, I stood with my eyes fixed upon the dark body of the coach, as for half a minute or so it rocked and swayed against the sky-line; then, with a subdued shout from the men, it suddenly disappeared. A moment later, from far beneath came a mighty crash of woodwork and the sharp tinkle of shivered glass.

George Woodley groaned, and ground his teeth with rage. But for the fact that we were still chained together and I held him back, I believe he would have rushed upon the gang and fought them with his bare hands.

"The murderous villains!" he muttered. "Fancy throwing a stage-coach into the sea, as if it were nothing more than an old fish-basket!"

"Steady, George," I whispered. "Keep your mouth shut. We're in the hands of these men, and they'll stop at nothing now to get their liberty. Be thankful they didn't knock us on the head at the first, or leave us tied to a tree to perish with the cold."

Once more the men instinctively formed a group round their leader, to learn what should be done next.

"I expect they're all abed in the village by this time," said Lewis; "still, there's nothing like making sure. There's a little place hereabouts where the rest of you can lie snug while I go down and put the oars in the boat, and see that all's quiet."

At the mention of the boat I pricked up my ears. Was it possible that some smuggling lugger was then off the coast, and that the gang were going straight on board? If so, what was to become of Woodley and myself? Surely they would not want to carry us with them across to France! In another hour, perhaps, we should regain our liberty.

A short distance away was a cavity in the ground—a sort of dried pit surrounded and overhung by gorse bushes. Into this, by Lewis's direction, we all crept, and lay or squatted in a huddled mass upon the ground. It was bitterly cold; my teeth chattered, and I was glad enough to creep close to George Woodley for the extra warmth. If Rodwood had been allowed to carry out his intention of binding us to a couple of trees in the lonely copse, the pair of us must certainly have been frozen stiff by morning. I could only hope that the shelter of the cottage and the warmth of the straw would preserve the warders and Tom from a similar fate.

It still wanted more than an hour to midnight, yet it seemed as if the darkness must have lasted a week, and I could hardly bring myself to believe that it was but a few hours since I had left the shelter of the Sportsman.

The convicts began to talk to each other in low tones, the chief topic of conversation being the likelihood of pursuit. Would the disappearance of the coach from the highroad have been discovered by now? This might or might not be the case. Breakdowns sometimes occurred which caused delay, and in case of anything serious the guard sometimes rode forward on one of the horses to obtain assistance.

"They must have been expecting of us at the stage beyond Tod's Corner," said one fellow; "and most likely after a time they'll send a man back as far as the last stopping-place. He'll hear we passed there all right, and then the question'll be what's become of us." The speaker chuckled, as though picturing to himself the astonishment of the stableman when it dawned on him that a coach and four, with guard, driver, and passengers, had apparently vanished into thin air, at some spot on the ten or twelve miles of dark, lonely road over which he had just ridden.

"It's bound to come out some time," answered a voice which I recognized as Rodwood's; "but it'll take time. Granted that the man has ridden back by now and found out that we're gone—well, what's he going to do? He and the rest will waste another hour talking; or perhaps they'll wait for the mail to come along, and tell the folks on that what's happened. Then it's ten to one they'll take it for granted that we've made off further inland. No; we're safe enough at present. With anything like luck we ought to have a fair start till morning."

Hardly had the words been uttered when there came a warning "Hist!" from some member of the gang whose sense of hearing must have been particularly acute. Men who go in constant peril of losing their liberty need no second hint of the presence of danger, and at once a deathlike silence prevailed. So infectious was the suppressed excitement that I felt the strain as much as if I myself had been an escaping prisoner. My heart thumped, and I held my breath, eager to ascertain the cause of the alarm.

For some moments I heard nothing; then, distinct and not far distant, there was a metallic tinkle as of a light chain. A pause followed, and then the sound was repeated, this time nearer to the pit, while at the same instant an exactly similar noise came from some little distance away in the opposite direction. On that wild spot, at such an hour, any sound not attributable to the wild animals or the forces of nature might have awakened the listener's curiosity; but in the present instance it was calculated to arouse something more than idle speculation. Not a man moved—they sat or crouched like figures of stone; and once again came that ominous jingle, exactly like the sound that might be caused by the movements of a man whose limbs were fettered.

"*It's the 'screws'!*" exclaimed one fellow in a horrified whisper, with that morbid superstition which is sometimes found in criminals. "This frost has done for them, and now they're following us with their ghosts!"

"Shut your mouth, you fool!" replied his companion fiercely. "If that's living men after us with the 'ruffles,' they won't put 'em on me! I'll make a few more ghosts before that happens!"

It was evident that the whole party had arrived at the same conclusion—that, by some means or other, they had already been tracked down by pursuers and their whereabouts discovered. How this could have happened it was impossible to imagine; but there was no mistaking that sound—more than one person was moving towards us on the common, incautiously allowing their approach to be heralded by the jingling of chains. For the moment I think even Rodwood forgot the presence of George Woodley and myself; but even if the thought had occurred to either of us to do such a thing, it would have been madness for us to shout or give any signal betraying our whereabouts, as we should certainly have paid the penalty of our lives for such an act.

The sharp tinkle sounded first on one side of the pit, and then on the other. Noiselessly Rodwood thrust his head forward into the centre of his followers.

"They're coming up on both sides," he whispered. "It's that man Lewis has done it," added the speaker, with an imprecation. "He's informed, to get his own liberty. This is a trap; but they won't take me out of it alive! Now, lads, no backing out. There are ten of us, and if we all strike together we'll prove a match for them yet!"

The words were followed by a click indicating the cocking of a pistol, and I noticed that the man nearest to me was working at a fragment of rock, endeavouring to dislodge it for use as a weapon.

At any other time I think I should have openly contradicted this charge of treachery against the absent man. Comparatively little as I knew of Lewis, I felt sure that whatever his faults might have been, he was never untrue to his own code of honour. I was, however, wise enough to hold my tongue, for a word uttered just then had like to have been the last I had ever spoken.

The clinking noise came nearer. There were long pauses between each repetition of the noise, as though the bearers were advancing cautiously, intending, when they got within easy distance of the pit, to carry the position with a final rush. Now on either side of us they appeared to be close at hand; the fateful moment had surely arrived, and my heart seemed to stop beating. The rascal at my side had loosened his jagged stone, and was clutching it with murderous intent; while the rest of the gang crouched, ready to spring to action at a signal from their leader.

Then suddenly the man named Nat broke out into a roar of hoarse laughter. The noise was, I think, more of a shock to the overstrained nerves of his comrades than a dozen pistol-shots. They sprang to their feet with a perfect howl of pent-up excitement. The next instant I fully expected their pursuers would leap down upon us, and the pit become the scene of a fierce conflict. Instinctively I shrank back under the overhanging bushes; but, to my surprise, nothing happened.

"Ho, ho!" burst out the voice of Nat above the confusion; "it's not the 'screws,' it's only some of those sheep! They chain them together out here on the coast, to prevent them straying."

"Keep quiet, you fool!" cried Rodwood. "D'you want to wake up every man in Rockymouth with your bull's roaring? Silence, you noisy hound, or I'll crack your skull with the butt of this pistol!"

However much inclined other members of the gang might have been to relieve their overstrung nerves with a laugh, Rodwood's threat was enough to force them into silence. One man sprung out of the hollow, and returned a moment later confirming Nat's statement regarding the sheep; and then, for the first time, I remembered having seen the animals on the cliffs, during my summer rambles with Miles, grazing in couples fastened together with collars and a chain, to hamper their movements and prevent their wandering.

It was certainly a ludicrous ending to what had seemed a tragic situation, but for my own part I was little inclined to laugh; and as the man beside me flung down his piece of rock, I could but feel thankful that the disturbance had proved a false alarm.

Once more the gang settled down to await the return of Lewis, who at length appeared with the intelligence that all was quiet in the village. With Rodwood and the old smuggler leading, and the rest of the party following in a straggling line, we made our way across the common and down a steep slope on the seaward side of the village. As George Woodley and I stumbled along over the uneven ground the handcuffs jerked, and chafed our fettered wrists; but the chance of our giving them the slip in the darkness and rousing up a pursuit was too serious a risk for the convicts to make it likely that they would liberate us at that important moment of their escape. On we went in perfect silence, skirting the village; and now almost immediately beneath us lay the harbour, sheltered from the beat of the open sea by the curved stone jetty, which always reminded me of a defending arm, crooked at the elbow, shielding the small craft which sought its protection. They had no need of it on this particular night, for the sea could not have been calmer if the month had been June instead of December.

Close behind me came the man whom I had seen helped down from the roof of the coach; and now, from a muttered word uttered now and again, I gathered that he was blind. Assisted, however, as before, by a comrade, he kept pace with the rest, and gave less trouble than might have been expected. We were half-way down the precipitous hillside when the leaders came to an abrupt halt—an example followed immediately by the rest of the party—and as we steadied ourselves, digging our heels into the ground, a voice cried,—

"Listen!"

It was the blind man who spoke. He had already uttered the word once before in a lower key, and I knew now that it was he who had given the first warning of the tinkling chains as we crouched in the pit.

As I have already said, the sea was very calm; there was no surf beating on the rocks, and in addition to this it was one of those still, frosty nights when the slightest sound can be heard with great distinctness. Sharp and clear, as though not more than a hundred yards distant, came the rhythmic clatter of a galloping horse. It was probably still the better

109

part of a mile distant, descending the long, steep hill to the village; but the sides of the valley threw back and intensified the sound, so that an impression was given of the rider being close at hand. It was not likely that any one would gallop at headlong speed into Rockymouth at close on midnight on a winter's night unless his business was urgent; and it did not take the escaped prisoners long to find a reason for the messenger's hot haste.

"The murder's out!" cried Rodwood. "They've guessed the direction we've gone in from the wheel-tracks. Now we shall have every dog in the county set at our heels!"

"It's one of the riding officers has got the news, I'll warrant!" answered Lewis.—"Come on, lads! only a nimble pair of feet will save you."

"Forward!" cried the man who now acted as our guard, at the same time giving George and myself a shove which nearly sent us headlong down the slope, while the whole party went plunging recklessly from ridge to ridge after the fleet-footed smuggler. Once, as Woodley made a false step, I thought my right wrist was broken, but we were too well aware of the mood of our companions to show any signs of hesitation. Gaining the level ground, we rushed on past the few cottages which straggled out towards the sea; the men, careless now of the noise their heavy boots made on the rocky ground, tore along, thinking only of speed, and for the most part believing that the horseman was close at their heels. Another moment, and we were stumbling breathlessly into the boat which Lewis had already drawn alongside the jetty. Down she sank under the unaccustomed load, until it seemed to me the gunnels were almost level with the water; then the damp stone wall began to recede—Lewis had pushed off—and the next instant the oars were grinding in the rowlocks.

Slowly we gathered way, and cleared the end of the pier; a gentle heave betokened the open sea, and as we felt it a shouting was heard in the village.

"We've got a start, anyway," muttered Lewis, who was bending his back to a long, steady stroke.

"Hullo!" exclaimed one of the men, "there's a dog crouching under this seat. How did he get in the boat, I wonder?"

"Let him be," answered the smuggler. "He won't do no harm. He's mine, and met me in the village. He'd only sit and howl if we left him ashore."

Hardly had the words been uttered when the boat gave a sudden violent lurch, which brought the water rushing in over the side. Had not George and I flung ourselves promptly to starboard, and thus brought all our weight to bear in the opposite direction, the overloaded craft would certainly have capsized, and flung all its occupants into the sea. In his excitement the convict who had taken the second oar had "caught a crab," and thus narrowly escaped bringing the adventures of the whole party to an untimely termination.

"You lubber!" growled Lewis.—"Isn't there a man among you who can pull an oar?"

"I can row if you'll free my hand," I exclaimed, not relishing the prospect of a watery grave, which was inevitable if this boatload of landsmen were once overturned.

"Yes, Master Eden, you'll do; I've seen you in a boat before," was the reply.—"For any sake cast off the boy's irons, some of you, and let him come forward."

Feeling rather proud, I fancy, as a boy might in proving himself superior to a number of grown men, I changed seats, and bent with a will to the oar, keeping time with the swing of Lewis's figure, which was dimly visible in the gloom. Thus the boat crept out to sea, and turning moved in a westerly direction down the coast.

There was no sign or sound of pursuit; our departure from the harbour had evidently not been discovered. I was too much occupied with my oar to notice where we were going; but at last, when my arms were beginning to ache, and

I feared I should have to ask to be relieved, Lewis ceased rowing, bidding me do the same; then turning, to my surprise I found we were close to shore, while above us towered the face of a mighty cliff.

Flinging his oar over the stern, with a skilful twisting of his wrist the old sailor sculled the boat carefully towards the towering mass of rock. In another moment I thought we should strike, and prepared involuntarily for the expected shock; then a half-circle of blackness resolved itself into the narrow, tunnel-like mouth of a cave.

Gently we drifted through the opening, a man in the bows guiding us with his hand, until the darkness became absolutely impenetrable, and the intense stillness was broken only by the lapping of water against the sides of the cavern.

This, then, was Lewis's promised hiding-place, and his assertion that there would be no danger of the men being found seemed no idle boast.

CHAPTER XII.

WITHIN THE CAVERN.

"Hi there! one of you men forrard, light the lamp!" said Lewis, ceasing in the motion of sculling. "Let's see where we're going."

His voice sounded strange and hollow, like that of a person speaking under an archway; and a rumbling echo of his words came back from the distance, showing that the cave was of considerable extent.

Rodwood had plundered a tinder-box from one of the warders, and the next moment the oarsman's request was responded to with the *click, click* of flint and steel. Even the strong glare of the big coach lamp did little more than reveal the surrounding darkness; the black water flashed and sparkled, and as the beam of light was directed from side to side the walls of the cavern loomed up out of the gloom. As yet there was no sign of the end of the cave, which was of a size altogether out of proportion to its narrow opening. It was lofty as well as long, and from the manner in which the walls went down perpendicularly into the sea, I imagined that there was a good depth of water beneath our keel.

"Turn the light ahead!" ordered Lewis, and once more the sculling oar was set in motion.

Slowly we penetrated farther and farther into the mighty foundation of the great cliff; then suddenly there was a bump, which shook us on our seats. I thought at first that the boat had grounded on a rock; but she gathered way again, though with something grating against her side.

"Hullo!" came from the man who was acting the part of lookout in the bow; "there's something floating in the water."

The lamp was brought to bear, and a number of dark objects were discovered alongside.

"It's wreck-wood," said Nat, leaning over the gunwale and grasping the end of a broken spar. "There's quite a lot of

113

it, and cargo too. That over there looks like the top of a barrel."

Lewis bent down and examined the floating *debris* with a critical eye.

"The set of the current brings a good bit of driftwood in here," he mumbled, "specially after a south-easterly gale. Hum! that's bad," he continued, as something seemed to catch his eye. "Looks uncommon as if one of the boats had gone ashore, or maybe been driven on Sawback Reef. It was blowing hard a week back; I could tell that even in the jail at Welmington."

Once more the boat moved on, a slight jar every now and then bespeaking the presence of more wreckage; then a shout from the lookout warned us that we had reached the end of our journey.

The cavern terminated in a platform of rock raised some six or eight feet above high-water level, and having a surface which might in all have afforded as much space as the floor of a fairly large sized room; some niches and ledges in the side of the cavern formed a sort of rude natural staircase from the water's edge, while a rusty iron ring seemed to show that boats had been moored there before.

"Now then, up with you!" said Lewis. "But mind what you're about. There's water running down from the roof which makes the rock uncommon slippery."

There being no longer any chance of our giving them the slip, and perhaps mindful of the service I had rendered in manning the second oar, the convicts seemed once more fairly well disposed towards George and myself. One of them lent me a hand as I clambered up the rock; another performed a similar service for Woodley. The hamper, the dead game, and the two lamps were transferred to the platform from the boat, and Lewis made fast the painter. The dog had scrambled up the rocks almost as soon as the boat touched. He had evidently been there before.

"Well, I'm hungry," cried one man; "I could chaw a leather strap! Just open that basket."

"Can't we start a fire?" inquired another fellow, whose teeth were chattering loudly. "I'm perished with the cold. There's wood enough in the water to burn for a week; and though it is wet, if we use the dry straw and the hamper for kindling, we shall be able to make a start, and once having done that, it'll be easy enough with a little care to keep going."

Numbed and chilled to the bone, the prospect of warmth seemed to appeal to the majority of the gang even more strongly than the necessity for food, and under Rodwood's direction they set to work to prepare fuel for a fire. In order that the hamper itself might be broken up for kindlings, it had first to be emptied of its contents, which were found to consist of a good-sized turkey, some mince-pies, a small cheese, some sausages, and a quantity of apples; also the bottle of wine which had not yet been opened. So utterly incongruous and out of place did this Christmas fare appear when exposed to view in that sea cavern, under circumstances so extraordinary, that the group of onlookers gave vent to their feelings with a burst of laughter.

"I take it wery kind of the folks as packed the 'amper for this 'ere picnic," said one of the convicts. "They evidently remembered my weakness for sarsengers!"

A long fissure in the rock, which was henceforth known as the "cupboard," afforded a suitable place for stowing away the provisions; and a tarred plank having in the meantime been fished out of the water, one burly fellow proceeded to split it into small pieces with the aid of a large clasp-knife belonging to George. A fire was soon kindled in the centre of the platform, more wreckage was collected by Lewis in the boat, and either heaped on the blaze or piled around it to dry. The sight of the crackling flames seemed to have an immediate cheering effect on the men, who gathered round, warming their numbed hands and exchanging jokes on the subject of their escape.

"Now then," exclaimed their leader, as the fire began to burn clear on one side, "make a spit, some of you, and bring along that turkey. You don't expect a party of gentlemen to eat it raw like a pack of starving dogs, I suppose?"

Some of these jail-birds seemed to have a wonderful knack of making the most of any material which might come to hand. Utilizing some pieces of wreck-wood, shaped roughly with the clasp-knife, they rigged up a kind of spit, which promised at least to prevent the necessity of our devouring the turkey raw. At the same time Lewis took the dipper from the boat, and placed it in such a position that it caught the thin trickle of fresh water which, as has already been mentioned, ran down one side of the rock.

I thought then, and have done so many a time since, how little the unknown person who packed that hamper imagined how and by whom the provisions which it contained would be consumed! Possibly it was the gift of the wife of some gentleman farmer, intended as Christmas cheer for some relative in the town. Now, instead of reaching its destination in the ordinary manner, it was supplying the needs of a band of outlaws in the fastness of a sea cavern.

There was nothing particularly appetizing about the half-cooked meat divided up with the big blade of a pocket-knife, and subsequently conveyed to the mouth with the fingers; but I myself felt ravenous, after the riding, tramping, and rowing in the cold night air. I was glad enough to receive my portion of the bird, and to eat it without the accompaniment of bread or even salt. The water in the dipper was heated over the fire, and wine added from the remaining bottle. The negus had, to be sure, a brackish flavour, but it sent a glow of warmth through our chilled bodies, and when the bowl was emptied a second brew was demanded.

At length the strange meal ended, and Rodwood ordered the lamp to be extinguished.

"It won't burn for ever," he said, "and we may want the light before we've finished."

With their faces illumined only with the flicker of the fire, the convicts gathered round to get as much warmth as possible, Woodley and I being forced to join the circle for the same reason; while old Joey retired to a corner, and there crunched up the bones and fragments which had been flung to him by the men.

Being but a boy, I think I was to a certain extent fascinated by the strangeness of the adventure. It seemed as if I personally were sharing the excitements as well as the hazards of the escape, though in my case there was no sense of guilt to lie heavy on my conscience. I might have been a prisoner wrongfully convicted making a dash for liberty. The delusion was perhaps strengthened by the fact that up to the present the personal risk and danger I had run had not been very great. Of Rodwood I certainly felt afraid, regarding him as an unscrupulous ruffian; but the remainder of the gang, perhaps with the exception of Nat, I believed certainly bore us more good will than ill, and would set us at liberty again as soon as they could do so without endangering the success of their own plans.

So, in a comparatively tranquil frame of mind, I stretched my tired limbs on the rock beside Woodley, and listened to the conversation.

"Well, and how long do you reckon we're going to stay here?" demanded Nat.

"We can't stir to-morrow—that is, not in daylight," answered Rodwood; "and I'm not sure if it'll be safe to do so at night either. There'll be too sharp a lookout kept for some days to make it over safe for us to take our walks abroad."

"Why can't we stay here for a week," said one fellow, "until the chase has been abandoned? If the food runs short, we could get more some night from the village; at least," he added with a laugh, "I reckon I could find some if any one will put me ashore!"

"It's risky to stay too long," muttered Lewis.

"What d'you mean?" asked Rodwood sharply. "I thought you offered to find us a safe hiding-place where there'd be no danger."

"I said where there'd be no danger of being found."

"Then what other risk is there?"

"The chance of getting in without being able to get out," was the reply. There was a certain ominous sound in the speaker's voice which attracted every man's attention, and I noticed that George Woodley turned his head to listen.

"What's the good of beating about the bush?" growled one man. "Speak out plain, you fool!"

"Why," returned the smuggler, "what I mean is, you can't get in or out of this place with anything of a rough sea running. It's calm now, but there's no knowing how long the weather's going to hold this time of year. You can't expect to walk out of jail and get off without running risks; if you steer clear of one, you must take your chance of running into another. Here's a place where there's precious little chance of your being found, except by them who, at a word from me, would take care not to see you; but there's equal chance, if you stay here till a gale should happen to spring up, that you'll be missing till the day of judgment."

The truth of this assertion seemed to shock the group of listeners into a momentary silence. To myself the danger of our present position became at once evident, and a sense of fear chilled my heart as I listened to the lapping of the water and thought of what must be our fate if the slumbering sea awoke in fury, and the huge billows thundered through the mouth of the cave. There was little doubt but that in a storm the ledge on which we rested would be swept clean with the surges, and any living being seeking refuge there would soon be drawn into the surf and dashed to pieces against the sides of the cavern.

"What d'you propose to do, then?" inquired Rodwood.

"It's no use to stir abroad in daylight," answered Lewis; "we must wait here till to-morrow night. Then I thought I'd go alone into Rockymouth, and try and get a word with them as will help us. They'll say how soon there's a chance of our getting across the water. I'll bring back some more food; and if I see any sign of bad weather, why, we must get out of this, and find some snug hole among the bushes on the cliffs. Maybe during to-morrow all that ground will be searched, and folks won't trouble to look there again."

For a few seconds the leader of the gang remained thinking, with his chin resting on his hand; then I saw him raise his head and dart a quick glance at Lewis.

"See here!" he exclaimed; "how are we to know that when you once get among your friends you'll ever come back again? I don't suppose there's a man among us who can swim; and if the fact of our being left behind should happen to slip your memory, here we should remain, like rats in a drain-pipe, to either starve or drown."

"When my word's given I don't go back on it," replied Lewis. "If you doubt me, you can send a man along with me in the boat."

"There, there, my friend! don't get angry," replied Rodwood with a laugh. "You've served us well in the past, and there's no reason to doubt you in the future; but when a man has knocked about the world as much as I have; he gets to look at a thing from more than one point of view."

Overcome at length by the fatigues and excitements of the day, and rendered still more drowsy by the grateful warmth of the fire, I

CHAPTER XIII.

THE BRANDY KEGS.

A vague sense of pain and discomfort at length began to enter into my dreams, and soon I awoke to find that, from having lain so long in one position on the hard rock, I was aching in every limb as though I had been beaten. For a moment or so my head swam with bewilderment as I stared about me and wondered where I was. It was like the recovering of consciousness after a fall. But presently the full recollection of the previous day's adventure flooded my memory. I struggled into a sitting posture, and gazed around. The sun had risen, but the mouth of the cavern being so small and far distant, the surrounding objects were visible in a sort of gray twilight, such as might have illumined some underground dungeon with but a single small barred window high up in the wall. The other members of the party were already astir—one man mending the fire, another plucking one of the pheasants we had brought with us, and a group of two or three hauling up more of the wreck-wood out of the water on to the platform.

Looking towards the mouth of the cave from where I sat was much like surveying the interior of a modern railway tunnel which by some means had become flooded, except that the cavern was more lofty. The roof itself was lost in darkness; but as far as I could make out, exactly over our ledge was a wide hole in the rock, like the perpendicular shaft of an old-fashioned chimney. This, however, was only discernible by the space of denser black amid the general gloom.

Shivering with the cold, I was glad enough to get some warmth by assisting in building up the fire. The broken spars which had been recovered the previous night were dry by this time, and made good fuel, of which there seemed a sufficient supply to more than last out our needs. There being no beach for nearly a mile on either side of us, a quantity of flotsam, as Lewis explained, was often to be found in the cavern, carried there by the current.

Our breakfast was a frugal one—a sausage and a small hunk of cheese served out to each man—Rodwood having determined to husband the food supply. Then the gang settled down to endure as best they could the long hours of waiting till it would be safe for Lewis to venture forth and bring back such information as would enable them to decide on their further movements.

From the time I awoke, the unpleasant conviction began gradually to force itself on my mind that the attitude and disposition of the escaped prisoners towards George and myself was undergoing a change. In the first glow of their gratitude for the small kindnesses and services which we had shown them, they had gone to an extreme in their expression of good will, but now a reaction became evident. Any obligation to us which they might have felt on the previous evening was now forgotten. They began to resent our presence among them, and appeared to regret that they had not taken their leader's advice, and not hampered their escape by bringing us with them to the coast. As far as was possible in such a limited space, they excluded us from their society, allowing us to have no share in their conversation, which, for the most part, seemed to turn on the various misdeeds for which they had suffered.

"What's to be done with 'em when we get out of here?" I heard one man remark.

"That'll be seen when the time comes," answered another. "I don't suppose they'd thank us to take 'em with us over to France."

On comparing notes with George, I found he had already remarked the same thing, but had refrained from mentioning it for fear of causing me unnecessary alarm.

"Laugh every now and again as if we were talking about something comic," he whispered as we sat together, a little apart from the rest. "It won't do to let 'em think we suspect them or notice any change."

So with many feigned grins and chuckles we continued our talk, though Heaven knows I never in my life felt less in a laughing mood.

"What d'you think they'll do with us?" I asked.

"How can I tell?" he answered. "But any one could see that there's rocks ahead for you and me. Put yourself in their place, and leave everything out of the question but your own safety, and think what's to be done. Once give us our freedom, and how are they to know that we shan't loose the dogs on their heels the very next minute? Another thing: if they take us with them, we shall be able to identify the men who help them in their escape—the crew of some smuggling craft, I expect—and it's not likely, with that knowledge in our heads, we shall be left to walk straight off to the nearest justice of the peace."

"Then what will they do with us? They can't leave us here; that would be worse than downright murder."

"There's no knowing what they'll do," answered George evasively.

"Old Lewis will remain our friend," I replied. "I'm sure he'll not stand by and allow us to come to harm."

"But what's he to do by himself, one to nine?" was the reply. "These are desperate men, and prepared for desperate measures. We're about as safe here, Master Eden, as if we were in a den of tigers."

"But Lewis can say, as he did before, that he won't help them if harm comes to us," I persisted, unwilling to abandon this sheet anchor of hope.

"He may say that once too often," muttered George. "You must remember, too, that the man's walking the greasy pole himself, so to speak, and one slip sends him down into transportation for life; for I don't doubt but what they'd all get that after this attempted escape and making away with the coach."

As one or two of the convicts seemed to be eyeing us, we ceased our conversation with a forced laugh; and rising, I strolled over towards Lewis, who stood at the edge of the platform with arms folded, gazing towards the mouth of the cave. If not then low water, the tide could not long have turned, and the ledge seemed considerably higher above the sea than it had done when we had first landed from the boat.

"What's the matter?" I asked, seeing how the old sailor's heavy brows were contracted in thought.

"There's a good bit may be the matter, Master Eden, before this gang of lubbers steps ashore in France," he answered. "I've been as far as the mouth of the cave this morning in the boat, and I don't altogether like the look of the sea: there's a swell getting up which may mean wind behind it. If so, these blokes may find this cave as difficult a place to get out of as Welmington Jail."

Now that he called my attention to it, I noticed that there was certainly a constant ripple whispering down the length of the cave. The boat rocked gently at her mooring, and at the sight of her a sudden foreboding of evil entered my mind.

"You don't think it's going to be rough enough to wash us off this rock?" I asked anxiously.

"I doubt if that would happen unless it came on to blow a regular gale," he answered. "You see, the mouth of the cave is only a narrow opening, and, especially at high water, the seas would spend most of their force outside; still, as I've warned these men here, if once a big storm did get up, not a mother's son of them is ever likely to be heard of again. No," continued the speaker, "it's not being drowned I'm so much afraid of now as there being just enough sea running to prevent us getting out. These fools don't realize what a ticklish job it is except in still water. Let them try it in a stiff sou'-easterly breeze, and see how far they get! I'll wager my neck not one of them would ever set foot on shore again."

I stood gazing anxiously at that distant semicircle of light beyond which the sea was sparkling in the wintry sunshine. As I did so a fresh salt breeze swept through the cavern, and a miniature wave rolled up and spent itself against the mass of rock on which we stood. I was on the point of making some further remark to Lewis, when, in a sharp, peremptory manner, a voice behind us exclaimed,—

"Hark!"

The hum of conversation going on round the fire instantly ceased, while Lewis and I involuntarily turned sharp round to see who had spoken.

"Hist! D'ye hear anything?"

It was the blind man who spoke. His name was Mogger, and he sat a little apart from his companions, with his back against the rock wall of the cavern. From chance remarks let drop by the others, I gathered that he had been accustomed to beg for his bread with a dog, leading-string, and tin can. Associating with a set of rogues and vagabonds, he had at length become concerned in a robbery, and had been found guilty of receiving and concealing stolen goods. His loss of sight appeared to have been in a measure made up to him by an abnormally keen sense of hearing; in fact, the fellow's ears were as sensitive to sound as a dog's. Walking down the middle of a road, he declared that he could tell whenever he passed a house, or when he emerged from between two rows of buildings into the open country, and this simply by the change in the sound of his own footsteps. I mention this as giving additional interest to the incident which I am about to describe.

There was a moment of dead silence. The picture of that scene rises in my mind now as I write—the blind man sitting bolt upright against the rock with closed eyes, and his pale, expressionless face raised at an unusual angle, as though an unseen hand had gripped him beneath the chin; the group round the fire, for the instant rigid and alert, with heads half turned and mouths opened in the attitude of listening; while Rodwood's hand closed instinctively on a pistol which he had been cleaning, and had laid beside him on the rock. Thus, in the gloomy twilight of the cave we all remained motionless as the rock itself, until one of the men broke the spell with speech.

"What's the matter now?—more sheep?" he demanded gruffly, referring to the false alarm of the previous evening, at which several of his companions laughed.

The blind man made no reply, but remained in exactly the same attitude, like a person in a trance. On any occasion his conduct would have been disquieting and uncanny, but for hunted men there was something in it especially disturbing.

"Can't you answer, you dumb post?" cried Rodwood angrily. "If you hear anything, tell us what it is."

"It was a voice," answered Mogger. "I heard it, I'll swear; my ears never play me false."

"You heard a good many voices, I suppose, seeing that we was most of us talking," retorted one of his companions, with an uneasy catch in the blustering tone which he tried to assume.

"I know all your voices," was the reply. "This was strange, and seemed to come from a distance. Hark!"

The man held up a warning hand. In the death-like stillness which followed I strained my ears to catch the faintest whisper; but no sound reached them save the plash of the water and the heavy breathing of Lewis, who stood close at my side.

"Be hanged to you!" burst out Rodwood. "You'll cry 'wolf' so often that we shall pay no heed to real danger when it comes. What you heard was the seagulls crying.— Confound the man, he's enough to send a nervous old woman into a fit with his prick ears and bladder face!"

The blind man seemed too intent in listening for a repetition of the sounds which he believed he had heard to take much notice of this speech. The convicts joined in a rough jeer, but it was evident that they had not recovered from the shock of the alarm.

"The dog's given no sign," said Lewis presently, looking hard at his four-footed companion. "He'd be uneasy if there was strangers about.—Eh, Joey? Is the coast clear?"

The animal merely wagged its tail, and before the subject could be discussed any further the attention of the party was diverted to another matter.

"Here's something in the water!" exclaimed one of the convicts, who had wandered to the edge of the platform. "Looks like a cask of some sort. Come on, and help to fish it out."

"If I were you I'd leave it where it is," interposed Lewis; "it'll bring you no luck."

"Why?" demanded the fellow, who was already clambering down the ledges of rock to get to the boat.

"Because it's dead men's property," answered Lewis. "It belongs to the crew of this boat that's been wrecked. They'll be coming to claim it if you don't leave it alone."

"Rubbish!" retorted the man. "Keep your sailor yarns for a ship's fo'castle!—Hurray, boys! See here! Call me a Dutchman if it isn't a keg of smugglers' brandy; and there's another bobbing about just over yonder!"

The group by the fire scrambled hastily to their feet, and I heard Lewis mutter a curse. He must have known all along what the kegs which we had seen floating in the water as we entered the cave really contained, and have foreseen the consequences of their coming into the possession of his companions. As it was, he stepped quickly from my side, and I saw him talking in quick, eager tones to Rodwood.

It would have been as easy to wrest a carcass from a pack of starving wolves as to rob this band of criminals of their newly-found store of liquor.

"Steady, lads, steady!" was all their leader could say. "One sup all round, and then let it rest; we shall need clear heads until we're safe out of the wood."

The words might as well have been spoken to the winds. The two ankers were quickly dragged up on to the platform, and one of them was broached with the aid of George's knife. The metal cup from the coachman's flask and a small mug found in the locker of the boat afforded the means of conveying the fiery spirit to eager lips. From hand to hand it passed. Rodwood himself, after some protestation, took his share with the rest, and even Lewis could not for long withstand the temptation of the liquor which was almost forced upon him. Woodley, however, was naturally a sober fellow, and kept his senses. He took one sip at the mug when it was handed to him, to avoid rousing the convicts to a still further feeling of hostility, after which he and I edged away from the rest, and sat down at the farther end of the platform.

What followed during the course of the next few hours it would be difficult to describe. The rousing of the appetite which they had for so long been unable to gratify was like applying a light to a heap of straw. Forgetful of food or of their perilous position, the men tossed the ardent spirit down their throats, and passed the cup for more. In a very short time the effect of the drink began to make itself evident, the more so that for some time past the members of the band had been forced abstainers. Their faces flushed, their eyes brightened with a feverish light, while with loosened tongues they began to jabber like monkeys, laughing long and uproariously at their own coarse jokes, and raising their voices to a shout when the din made it no longer possible for them to be heard.

There was no talk now of limiting the allowance; even Rodwood himself was far too intoxicated to care, while Lewis seemed robbed of that instinct of caution which had been bred in him by the risks of his calling.

How long this orgy lasted I don't know, but it must have continued far into the afternoon. The tide rose, and with it the sea; the broken waves seemed to come jostling and elbowing each other through the entrance to the cave, and splashed heavily against the foot of our platform, sprinkling the unheeding revellers every now and again with a dash of salt water. If the revenue cutter or any small craft had passed close in to shore, the noise made by the fugitives must have betrayed their whereabouts, as in their drunken frenzy they danced and yelled like raving lunatics.

At length, quite suddenly it seemed to us, they were all fighting. How the quarrel first started it was impossible to discern; but it had not been in progress more than a few seconds when all the band were engaged in the conflict. In terror I crouched in the corner of the rock farthest removed from this scene of strife, expecting momentarily to receive some injury from this outburst of unreasoning fury. With clenched fists, and with logs of wood snatched from the ground, the maniacs struck at each other, or grappling fell, and were trodden on and stumbled over by the other combatants. Rodwood, fighting like an enraged lion, and striking out indiscriminately right and left, felled several antagonists, and was ultimately the means of putting an end to the mêlée, but not before one man had received some severe injury from a kick in the stomach, and another had been horribly burned about the face from falling, half stunned, into the fire. The groans of these wretches now mingled with the maudlin peacemaking of the other members of the band, as they rubbed their bruises and gathered once more round the brandy keg.

The fading light of the short winter day was deepening into darkness as the horrid scene continued.

"Hark'ee!" cried Rodwood, suddenly dashing the pewter cup to the ground: "I've no mind to spend another night in this foxes' burrow. Let us go back to the little port yonder and say we're what's left of a shipwrecked crew. I'll be bound good beds enough would be offered to such jolly mariners!"

A babel of voices followed this proposal. Some men were in favour, while others, perhaps a trifle more sober, were against the move.

"I'd like to see you pass yourselves off as sailor men," shouted Lewis with a wild laugh. "Besides, who's going to get the boat out with this swell on? She'll be bottom up before she's ten yards beyond the opening."

A fresh outburst of drunken argument drowned his further remarks, and it soon became evident that the more reckless spirits had carried the day. The remaining keg of brandy was handed down into the boat, and the men prepared to follow, the first to move falling under the thwarts, where he lay yelling that his arm was broken, while his comrades staggered over his prostrate form.

George Woodley and I rushed forward. Whatever the risk of the voyage might be, it was preferable to being left behind. But as we approached the group of men who were gathered at the head of the flight of rough steps, Rodwood waved us back.

"No room for you!" he cried with an oath. "No strangers or informers come with us now; we've got enough to do to save our own necks."

"Quite right, captain!" added another drunken scoundrel. "Why did they come with us at all? Let them bide there till they're fetched."

"For mercy's sake don't leave us here!" cried George. But a blow in the face, which sent him staggering backwards, was the only response. The blind man and the fellows who had been injured in the fight were handed down into the boat. One groaned heavily as he was moved, his complaints rising at last to a shriek which made my blood curdle.

"Lewis! Lewis!" I shouted in despair, "tell them to make room! We won't betray you!"

The smuggler heard my cry, and paused with his foot already on the first step of the descent.

"It's no good, Master Eden," he said, in a low, thick utterance. "If I put you in the boat they'll throw you out. You're all right—I'll tell Master Miles; or if not, you'll find it yourself if you look about. I'm the only one as knows—"

The words, which I regarded merely as the rambling nonsense spoken by a drunkard, were cut short by the speaker being forcibly dragged down into the boat, which an instant later shoved off from the platform.

In an agony of despair we heard it receding farther and farther in the gloom, the hoarse shouts and laughter of the men and the continuous barking of the dog, which had sprung aboard at the last moment, echoing strangely from the arched roof. A few moments later we saw the dark outline of the overladen craft obscuring the semicircle of light as it reached the mouth of the cavern, and at the same time the drunken clamour seemed to end in one final yell.

The men were gone, and George and I were left to our fate, at the mercy of wind and sea.

Deserted.

CHAPTER XIV.

ABANDONED.

There was a pause as we stood in the deepening darkness at the end of that horrible tunnel. Cold, hungry, and despairing, I think if I had been alone I should have broken down completely; but George Woodley, though no doubt sharing to a great extent my own feelings, did his best for my sake to put as cheerful a face on the matter as was possible under the circumstances.

"Cheer up, Master Eden," he exclaimed. "While there's life there's hope, and we're a good way off being dead yet, sir. I shouldn't wonder," he continued, "if this doesn't turn out all for the best as far as we're concerned. These men, drunk as they are, will be certain to be captured as soon as they step ashore. Lewis will think of us and say where we are, and my belief is we shall be rescued to-morrow morning."

There certainly did seem some probability that things would turn out as the guard suggested; anyway, it was a ray of hope to lighten the gloom of our present situation. Still, the prospect of spending another night in that dark cavern, with the danger of the sea rising ever present in our minds, seemed almost unbearable.

"We mustn't let the fire out," said my companion. "There's that bird to cook, and I'm fairly famished."

I myself was faint with hunger, for, owing to the drunken outbreak among the convicts, we had spent the whole day since our scanty breakfast without food. The pheasant which one of the men had drawn and plucked had lain unheeded and forgotten since the appearance of the brandy kegs, and this we decided should form our evening meal.

Building up the fire and improvising a spit on which to roast the bird occupied our attention, and relieved our minds by diverting our thoughts from our forlorn and perilous position. We found the metal cup which Rodwood had flung down, and also the wine bottle, the neck of which had been broken off, and this we placed under a trickle of fresh water—the dipper having been carried off in the boat.

"The rascals have taken the coach lamp with them," said George. "We shall have to feel our way about as best we can."

Almost as he spoke my foot struck against something which slid along the rock with a metallic clatter, and stooping down, to my joy I picked up the guard's clasp-knife, which had also been overlooked by the drunken gang at the time of their departure. The find gave us considerable satisfaction, as the knife had proved of great service in many ways, and we were already contemplating the necessity of tearing the pheasant apart with our fingers.

The meal was no more appetizing than the one which had preceded it on the previous evening. How I longed for a morsel of bread and salt! The last defect I tried to rectify by dipping my meat in salt water; but the result was not all that could be desired, and Woodley laughed at the wry faces which I pulled.

However, the flesh of the bird, followed by a mince-pie, and an apple by way of dessert, certainly appeased our hunger, and in doing so enabled us to face our position with more fortitude. Reclining on the hard rock as near as we could get to the smouldering fire, we went over the whole of our strange adventure from the moment the convicts had seized the coach to the time they had left us in the boat.

"We might be worse off," said George. "I believe that if they'd tied us up in that copse, as that rascal Rodwood suggested, we should have been frozen stiff by morning. I wonder how poor Tom got on! That was a nasty fall of his; I heard his head strike on the hard ground, and I made sure he'd be picked up dead. Them warders, too—I hope the warmth of the straw and the shelter of the cottage kept them alive."

"I believe those villains would have killed any one who had tried to stop them," I remarked. "Do you remember that fellow close to me digging out that stone with his fingers in the pit on the cliff, when the sheep made that false alarm? The way he did it made me tremble. I believe he'd have brained some one with it if we really had been surrounded."

"Well, the whole lot of them are taken by this time, dead or alive; at least that's my belief," answered George. "They were crazy with drink, and would walk straight into the net. That man we heard gallop into the village last night may have given the alarm, and I'll wager there's been a hue and cry and a sharp lookout all to-day. As long as the sea don't prevent it, we shall have a boat sent here for us to-morrow, and then a fine story you'll have to tell the folks at home, and the boys at school next term, Master Sylvester!"

His last remark, though intended to cheer me up, had rather the opposite effect. I must confess that, up to the present, I had been so much concerned with my own personal safety as to give hardly a thought to the friends at home, and to the anxiety which my father and mother must be now feeling at my non-arrival; for by this time the news would no doubt have reached them of the disappearance of the coach. In those days there were no telegraph wires by means of which messages could be sent and replies received in the course of at most a few hours. A messenger had probably been dispatched on horseback to Round Green, to learn whether I had travelled by the ill-fated True Blue; but he would probably not return to Castlefield till late that night. And even now, as I sat blinking at the glowing logs, my parents would be in a state of anxious uncertainty as to whether I was really missing, or had been detained for some reason at the school.

George did not notice my silence, but went on, following up his own line of thought.

"I believe there's been a boat out to-day spying down the coast, and 'twas that the blind fellow heard when he talked about distant voices. My stars! it gave me quite a turn for the minute. I almost thought it was ghosts, and so did some of the rest, I suppose, by the scared look on their faces. You didn't hear nothing, I suppose, did you, Master Eden?"

"No," I replied. "But I hardly expected to; for I've got a bit of a cold in my head, and it's made me rather deaf."

"It was a queer thing," murmured George. "That man had such sharp ears I don't think 'twas fancy; and if not, then what could it have been, I wonder?"

"The dog didn't seem to notice it," I answered, "and a dog can hear better than a man. I dare say it was the water gurgling in some hole or hollow, and it may have sounded like a voice."

How endless seemed that long December night! The cold did not appear to be so intense, but I was less weary than on the previous evening, and less inclined for sleep. Every now and again Woodley would raise himself on his elbow to readjust the smouldering logs; and we would speculate as to what could be the time, for the man had forgotten to wind his watch the night before, and it had run down. We cheered each other with the assertion that the people in Rockymouth must know now of our whereabouts, and that when day dawned we should be rescued. At length we must both have fallen into an uneasy slumber, and when I recovered consciousness the mouth of the cavern was showing like a distant window in the pale gray light of morning. Rising, and stretching our stiffened limbs, we stirred up the fire, and slapped our arms across our breasts to restore the circulation. To my joy I noticed that the sea was calmer; the wind had dropped, and what waves there were outside reached our platform in little more than gentle ripples.

"They won't be long fetching us now," said George. "I wonder how far those rascals got before they were collared?

Not much farther than the pierhead, I fancy. The villains, sending the old *True Blue* over the cliffs like a worthless piece of rock! I hope they'll get a sound flogging for it, every man Jack of 'em, when they get aboard the hulk. I'd like to give it 'em myself!"

We stood watching the light strengthen in the entrance to the cave, momentarily expecting to see the aperture darkened by the prow of a boat, and prepared to give a simultaneous hail with all the force of our voices.

"Well, some of those lazy dogs of villagers might have been up and about by this time," grumbled George. "I know I would if it were a case of rescuing fellow-creatures in distress. They needn't have waited for dawn; I'll warrant there's some of them could have guided a boat in here with a lamp if there'd been a cargo of brandy kegs to be fetched, instead of two human beings!"

"Perhaps they don't know we're here," I suggested, rather reluctantly.

"Of course they do," answered George, who had fully made up his mind on the subject. "That gang of rascals must have been caught yesterday. How could it have been otherwise when most of them were too drunk to walk, let alone run? That being the case, for their own sakes they'd be ready enough to say what had become of us. They'll be held responsible for our safety, and it would go hard with them if—if we weren't found."

"But they might have got into hiding, and be waiting to get on board some vessel."

"Not they! The harbour was empty when we got into the boat—I noticed that; so there was no craft lying alongside the wharf which would take them on board, we'll say, and stow them down in the hold. No; they'd have to go ashore. It's risky enough for men who know their way about to beach a boat along this coast among the rocks and breakers, and especially after dark; and the only chance for these fellows would be to make the harbour and land on the quay. Bless you, they were too reckless and fuddled to think of the chances of being caught. They've all been nabbed safe enough, and had time by now to cool their heads and remember whom they left behind. We shall be taken off directly, and in the meanwhile I don't see why we shouldn't have breakfast."

I sat down readily enough, and ate my share of what was left of the pheasant, and a small wedge of cheese, washing down the repast with a draught of the fresh water in the broken bottle. Still there was no sign of the relief party, for the arrival of which we kept a constant lookout, and I thought I noticed an uneasy look on Woodley's face, which did not tend to allay my own misgivings.

Growing restless at this delay, we longed to be doing something, and at length decided to try to secure some more pieces of the floating wreckage. George was the first to rise to his feet, and as he did so he exclaimed,—

"Hullo! here's a find!"

Lying on the ledge of rock where Rodwood had left it on the previous evening was the warder's pistol. My companion examined it, and finding that it was loaded and primed, clambered up and put it in a niche of the rock high above his head, remarking as he did so,—

"There, that's safer than letting it lie about on the ground. A chance kick might send it off, and one of us get the ball in his foot."

The set of the current seemed to have drifted more wreckage into the cavern, and the flowing tide had brought a quantity of it close to the extreme end of the cave, where it floated in a jumbled mass at the foot of our platform. By clambering down to the water's edge and "fishing" with another broken spar, we had no difficulty in drawing it towards us and then throwing it up to the rock above. One piece of timber which seemed a portion of a mast had a quantity of rope attached to it, and a couple of blocks with more cordage were also secured. At length my eye rested on another of those mischievous kegs, but this one apparently half or wholly empty, judging from the manner in which the greater portion of it appeared above the surface of the water.

"There's another of those little barrels," I said to George, half jestingly. "Haul it out, and we'll use it as our water-butt."

The keg was accordingly fished out of the sea, and added to our little pile of salvage. One or two more small fragments of wood were next recovered; then George pointed to a long, slender spar which I had already noticed, but which was floating close to the opposite wall of the cavern, and beyond our reach.

"That looks like an oar, Master Eden," he said. "We'll get that somehow. I think I can manage it with a line and slip-knot made out of some of that rope."

It did not take long for this simple tackle to be prepared, and with its aid George soon secured the oar, and handed it up to me as I stood above him on the rock. He passed it up, I say, blade first, and I remember, as I caught hold of it, having given a sudden cry, almost as though the wood had been red-hot iron.

"What's the matter?" shouted the astonished guard.

"O George, look here!—look at this!"

With a bound Woodley was at my side; but even then he could not guess the reason for my outcry. There was, after all, little for him to see—merely a letter "L" branded into the water-worn surface of the wood.

"What's the matter?" he asked.

"Matter!" I cried. "Don't you see that mark? This is one of the oars from Lewis's boat. O Woodley! can't you guess what's happened? She's capsized, and all those drunken rascals are drowned. I remember now there was a yell as they passed out of the cave, and then silence. I thought they'd gone beyond our hearing, but when they got into the swirl of the backwash at the foot of the cliffs they must have overturned. Lewis himself told me how dangerous it was. It would have been a difficult thing for a sober and experienced crew to get safely out to sea, but with the first bad lurch those madmen would have flung themselves about, and lost their balance in no time."

"It can't have been that," said George, who stood aghast at my suggestion. "Ten men drowned within fifty yards of us, and we none the wiser! No, no, Master Eden; I won't believe it."

"You forget they were all of them drunk," I answered. "Even if any of them had floated for a moment, we weren't likely to hear their stifled cries right back here, and above the noise the wash of the sea was making."

"How d'you know that oar came out of the boat? Its being marked with an 'L' is no proof that it belonged to Lewis."

"You forget I went out in his boat several times last summer, and learned to row. I remember the oar as well as if it was my own; it's got a smaller 'L' carved with a knife just below the button. There, see for yourself."

Still George stood staring at me as though unwilling to be convinced that the worst had happened.

"Look at that keg," I continued, "and see if it isn't the one they took with them in the boat. If so, you'll find the small hole they made with your knife."

On examination, the spot where the convicts had broached the anker was clearly visible. There could no longer be any doubt as to how it came to be floating on the water.

"Some of them must have got to land," muttered George doggedly.

"Not they!" I replied; "there wasn't a man of them could swim. Don't you remember what Rodwood said? I know Lewis couldn't, because he told us so last summer; and we remarked at the time how strange it was he had never learned, when he had spent most of his life on the water. Besides, what difference does it make to a man whether he can swim or not, if he's flung into the water stupefied with drink?"

The oar dropped from my hands as I spoke, and for some minutes each stood staring blankly in the other's face. That short space of silence did as much as an hour's feverish discussion of the subject to impress upon our minds how hazardous and almost hopeless our position had now become. No gloomy underground dungeon in some ancient prison, made secure by locks and bolts and watchful jailers, could have afforded less chance of escape than in our case did this cavern; for even if a boat had been waiting close outside, as neither of us could swim, there was enough deep water between us and the sunshine to drown us twenty times over. It was probable that even the smugglers only entered the cave on rare occasions, for too frequent visits would draw attention to the spot; and especially at this time of the year, close on Christmas, the chances were a thousand to one against any boat coming near the place till we had either died of starvation or been washed away in one of the fierce storms which raged constantly during the winter months. With the loss of the boat and its occupants all chance of communication with the outer world was ended; and if we had been marooned on an island or coral reef in the Pacific, far out of the usual track of ships, there could hardly have been less prospect of a timely rescue.

Though all these thoughts flashed through our minds, we neither of us seemed willing to put them into words; both shrank from being the first to pronounce the sentence of our doom. George Woodley at length broke the silence, and he did so in a voice the tone of which betrayed strong emotion.

"This is a bad lookout for us, Master Eden," he said. "What are we to do?"

"We must portion out the food," I answered, "and make it last as long as possible. There's the other pheasant, and the hare, two or three mince-pies, and a few apples, and part of the cheese. With that we ought to keep from starving a few days longer."

George shook his head, as if to imply that it would be only lengthening the agony of our suspense; and for a time we remained doing nothing but listlessly watching the sparkling patch of sea beyond the mouth of the cavern, in the vague hope that some boat would pass within hail. Owing to the fact that the entrance arch was low, and our platform was raised some distance above the water level, our view of the outside world was very limited, and unless a boat had come close in to the foot of the cliff we could not have seen her.

How long we remained thus in a state of hopeless inactivity I cannot tell. The hours of daylight seemed hardly less long and dragging than those of darkness. Woodley sat by the fire nursing his knees and sullenly chewing a splinter of wood. At last he roused himself and stood up.

"It's no good sitting here like this and not making a single bid for freedom!" he exclaimed. "A thought's just come into my head, and if you can't suggest anything better, why, I vote we try my plan."

"What is it?" I cried eagerly.

"Why, it's this," he answered. "We must at least try to get outside where folks can see us, and we can cry for help. Neither of us can swim, but here's wood, and rope to fasten it together. Why shouldn't we make a raft?"

The proposal was one exactly calculated to appeal to a boy's imagination; but when I cast my eyes over our stock of timber, the possibility of putting the project into actual execution seemed almost out of the question.

"There's never enough wood here for that!" I answered.

"There may not be sufficient to make a raft that would carry us both, but there ought to be enough to keep one of us afloat. Look here, sir," continued the man earnestly: "we've got to get out of this place somehow, and the sooner the better. If it means running risks, why, we shall have to run them. We're in peril of our lives as it is, standing here upon this rock. If it should come to blow really hard to-night, it would be good-bye to us before morning. My idea is this:—We must fasten enough of these logs together to make a raft big enough to carry me. That oar will serve as a paddle, or to shove off from the rocks, and so doing I ought, at all events, to be able to get outside into open water; and once out there I should be bound either to be seen or to drift ashore somewhere where I could climb the rocks. Then, you may be sure, it won't be long before I bring a boat round to rescue you."

"O George," I exclaimed, "I don't think I can stand being left quite alone in this awful place! Besides, what if you are washed off into the sea? You can't swim."

"I must take my chance of that, sir, as you must of being left," was the answer. "I'd suggest your going, only I think I'm the stronger, and could hold on longer if, as is sure to be the case, the waves wash over the logs. Think, sir, what'll happen in the first gale, even if our food lasts, and then take your choice."

I glanced round at the dark walls of our prison, which, though now high and dry, had been worn smooth by the storms of ages; and the very thought of the mountainous seas forcing their way in irresistible fury through the entrance of the cavern made me shudder. Take a bottle three parts full of water, I thought, and shake it violently from side to side, and that, on an infinitely larger scale, might be taken to represent what the interior of this cave would be like in a winter storm.

"Very well," I answered desperately. "If that's your plan, let's carry it out; I know of none better."

He turned at once, and worked with feverish eagerness, as though we knew that the dreaded storm was then brewing. Every piece of wreckage of any size which still remained within reach we fished out of the water and added to our store. The next business was to collect and untangle the rope and cord, and this took us far longer than we expected. The sodden knots wore the skin off the ends of our fingers, and made the job all the more laborious and painful. It was late in the afternoon before this portion of our task was accomplished. Then came selecting the most suitable pieces of timber, and planning how they should be arranged and joined together. All this while we kept glancing anxiously towards the entrance of the cave, still hoping against hope that some of the convicts might have escaped a watery grave, and either by capture or giving themselves up have made known our whereabouts to the good folks of Rockymouth. No help arrived, however, and it became more and more evident that none was to be expected. The patch of sea grew gray and misty as the second day of our captivity drew towards its close.

Kneeling in the quickly-gathering darkness of the cavern, George completed the first lashing of the logs; then gathering up all the remainder of the rope, that we might not entangle our feet, he stowed it away high up on the rocky ledge which had served as a shelf for our provisions.

All day we had hardly thought of food—a bite of cheese while we worked having proved sufficient; but now, though wearied with our labour, we set to work to pluck and cook the second pheasant—an operation which, as we sat in the darkness with no means of telling how time was passing, seemed to last far into the night. With most of our wood gone to form the raft, we had to be chary of our fuel. The bird was only half cooked, and I had little inclination for eating; but we forced ourselves to swallow something, for on George's strength keeping up, if not on mine, our last chance of rescue depended.

My cold was worse, and I felt utterly miserable as I sat crouching by the glowing embers, the warmth from which was not sufficient to temper the bitter breeze from the sea, which swept through the cavern as through a draughty tunnel.

"George," I said, "it would be awful to die here alone in the dark, and no one ever to know what had become of us. Are you sure that raft will carry you safely?"

"Oh, bless you, Master Eden, don't talk about dying," answered the man; "that's not the way the true Briton looks at things. 'Never say die' is his motto. There's many poor fellows been in worse plights than we are, and not thrown up the sponge. Bless you, sir, I shall help to carry you to and from school many a time yet, I hope. 'Woodley,' you'll say, 'this is better than the two nights we spent in that cave!' 'You're right, sir,' I shall answer; and then all the other outsides'll want to hear the story. Ho, ho! my eye! but I doubt if they'll believe it's all true!"

He went on cheering me with his lively talk, though his teeth chattered with the cold. He had never seemed more gay when perched on the back seat of the old *Regulator*. Yet if I could have read his thoughts, I might have discovered that he more than half believed that this was to be his last night on earth; for though determined for my sake, as well as for the wife and child dependent on him, to attempt an escape from the cave by means of the raft, he did not doubt that the chances were very much against his ever reaching the shore. So, for the sake of the youngster at his side, he hid his fears and made light of the uncertain future. Such was George Woodley, and as such I like to remember him: on the highroad a mail-coach guard, in the presence of death a very gallant gentleman.

The day had been tiring as well as anxious, and in spite of cold and discomforts my heavy eyelids began at length to droop and my head to nod, until before long my troubles were swallowed up in blissful forgetfulness.

I must have slept some hours, totally unconscious of what was going on around me. I have a distinct recollection that I was dreaming of making a journey by coach as an inside passenger. Mile by mile we went rumbling on; it was windy, for the blast came in gusts through the open windows, and roared in the tops of the wayside trees. We stopped to change horses, and as I looked out an hostler lifted a pail of water and, with a shout, flung it in my face!

I awoke gasping and choking. The water and the shout had been no dream, nor, for that matter, the unceasing sound which had seemed to me the noise of the wind and the lumbering vehicle. The next instant my arm was seized and shaken by Woodley.

"Rouse up, Master Eden!" he cried; "rouse up, sir! There's a storm coming on, and the sea is splashing over the rock!"

CHAPTER XV.

IN DESPERATE STRAITS.

Dazed by the sudden alarm, I lay for a moment hardly knowing where I was; then another lash of icy cold water across my face brought me to my senses, and I sprang to my feet.

Never shall I forget those terrible moments as we stood in pitchy darkness, relieved only by the faint, uncanny, phosphorescent light of the sea-water. The thudding boom of a big wave striking against the cliff and bursting in through the narrow archway, then the peculiar hollow sound the water made as it rushed along the cavern, and the fierce splash with which it expended its force against our platform—all are sounds which seem to echo in my ears even now as I write.

"The wind's come at last!" shouted George, and added something further which I could not catch.

"We're safe here," I answered at the top of my voice.

"I've no idea what the time is," he replied; "but I don't believe it's high water yet—the tide's still rising."

For just a few moments I think even brave George Woodley was panic-stricken at our hazardous situation, and his words added a fresh terror to the darkness. If the tide was still flowing, then it was only a matter of waiting till we should be washed away and drowned. There was apparently nothing to be done but to take up our position as far back as the width of our platform would allow, and so remain till our fate was decided.

The air was full of a fine drenching mist, but as yet only the broken spray from the waves had reached us. Trembling with cold and terror I stood, hoping against hope that the tide had reached its height or begun to ebb; then suddenly a larger sea than had hitherto entered the cavern swept clean over our place of refuge, the rushing surf whirling and

146

hissing round our feet like a thousand serpents. The water had not taken us much above the ankles, but in that awful darkness I imagined for a moment that the end had already come, and clung to George with a cry of alarm.

"We must climb higher, Master Eden," yelled Woodley, his words, though shouted in my ear, almost drowned in the rush of the back-wash. "We must climb the rock; there's a ledge above us, if we can only get to it."

The words had hardly been uttered when, as though to enforce the necessity of his suggestion, another deluge of foaming surf swept over the rock, and I heard a clattering, bumping noise, the woeful significance of which I did not realize at the moment. Groping with our hands over the surface of the cold, slippery stone, and yelling directions to each other, though our heads were not two feet apart, we climbed precariously from one foothold to another till we reached a ledge some five or six feet above the level on which we had hitherto been standing. This was as far as we could get, for above us the end wall of the cave rose precipitously, as though the rock had been hewn to stand the test of line and plummet.

Weary, wet, and chilled to the bone, in such a miserable condition I think I would hardly have troubled to avoid a speedy ending to all my misfortunes if death had presented itself in a less terrible form. But the fearful churning of that wild water was sufficiently appalling to cause one to cling with frenzied earnestness to any position of safety; for to be drawn down into that raging tumult was as dreadful to contemplate as being flung bodily into some enormous piece of whirling machinery, to be ground and dashed out of all human shape by a force as pitiless as it was overwhelming.

Higher and higher rose the tide. Now our platform was completely awash, and the seas, dashing against the end of the cavern, leaped up like hungry wolves, and soaked afresh our already sodden clothes with icy water. Thrown back in echoes from the arched roof of the cave, the noise of the sea

147

was probably magnified tenfold, and in the darkness was terrifying to hear, while the compressed air rushed through the opening above us with a long, whistling sigh. The wonder seems to me that the pair of us did not lose our reason. Happily for us, in those days folks were evidently made of tougher material, both as regards muscle and nerve, else I could hardly have survived the exposure of that night, let alone its long agony of suspense. As it was, I had come about to the end of my tether; and had it not been for Woodley, I should never have survived to write the present story. There came a boom louder than we had heard before. I seemed to feel that mighty mass of broken water sweeping towards us through the gloom. Then with a crash it burst over the lower ledge, and rose level with our armpits. I felt my numbed fingers relaxing their hold, and with a wild, despairing cry was slipping from my place, when Woodley seized me with one arm round the waist as the water subsided with a deafening roar.

That sea, I believe, was the largest which swept through the cave, and shortly after this the tide must have commenced to ebb; but of what happened next I had positively no remembrance, nor, strange to say, had George. Whether he held on to me after I lost consciousness, or whether we both continued to cling with a blind instinct of self-preservation to our ledge when our overtaxed brains had become oblivious to our surroundings, I cannot tell. How we maintained our foothold through the succeeding hours of darkness is a mystery. The next recollection I have is of finding myself lying on my side on the platform, staring blankly at the tossing surf as it rushed through the distant arch of rock in the gray light of morning.

The sea was rough, and a strong wind was blowing; but terrible as it had seemed at high water and in the darkness of night, it could not have been more than what seamen term half a gale, or we must certainly have been swept away and drowned.

I was so numbed that it was with great difficulty I could move my stiffened limbs and stagger to my feet; and when George spoke to me I discovered that I was nearly deaf—a result probably due to aggravation of the cold from which I had previously been suffering. What sort of an object I myself presented I have no means of telling, but when I looked at George I was shocked at his woebegone appearance. His face was haggard and pinched with cold, and something of that long night of terror seemed to remain in the wild glitter of his eyes. His cap was lost, and his sodden and dishevelled clothing hung about him like rags. Becoming aware of the fact that I was looking at him, he pointed, mutely with his finger. I saw in a moment what he meant; and if it had been possible for hope and courage to sink lower in my breast, they would surely have done so then. The sea had made a clean sweep of the rocky platform, and the raft was gone!

Save one piece of splintered board, which the waves had wedged into a fissure of the rock, not a fragment of wood remained in our possession; and not only had the wreckage been washed away from the spot where we had stored it, but the retreating tide, and some change in the currents, seemed to have carried it once more out to sea. I had reached a condition of despair and misery far beyond that which can find relief in tears; I could only stare in a dull, stupefied fashion at the empty space of cold, wet rock.

Woodley said something, but I could not catch his words.

"Speak louder," I answered, in a voice as hoarse as a crow's. "I can't hear; I believe I'm going deaf."

"All the timber's gone—every inch," cried George, coming nearer. "I've been having a look round, and there's nothing left but a lump of cheese and a bundle of rope what's up there in the 'cupboard.' I'm afraid we've played our last card, Master Eden."

I knew what he meant. If the sea continued rough, as there was every probability of its doing, we should never be able to hold out a second time when the tide rose and once more flooded our refuge. The misery and mental anguish through which we had passed had, I think, gone far to rob us both of the fear of death; but the form in which it appeared was terrible to contemplate, and the longing for life still throbbed fiercely in our breasts.

I said nothing; but feeling the water squelching in my boots, I emptied them, and then began stamping my icy feet in order to restore the circulation. Was there no hope? Must we remain like condemned criminals watching the angry water slowly rising till it claimed its prey? Of escape there seemed no possible chance, but in the anguish of our desolate condition I prayed fervently to God for fortitude and consolation to support us in our last hours.

Making cups of our hands, we drank from the trickling water as we ate our cheese. We had little to say to each other; even George seemed to have abandoned hope, and to be nerving himself up, that when the time came he might make a brave ending and encourage me to do the same.

"It seems months since I took you up at the Sportsman, Master Eden," he said, after a long silence. "Ah me! you little expected you was starting on such a queer journey."

He spoke in so kind and gentle a manner that I knew instinctively his thoughts and regrets were more for me than for himself. Somehow his tone, and the memories which his words awakened of the many times I had clambered up beside him on those happy days when I had returned to the home and dear ones I should never see again, broke me down; and rising hastily, I went forward to the edge of the platform and stood there, vainly endeavouring to stifle my sobs. I was but a boy, and am not ashamed now to remember those emotions.

I must have stood like this for some time, when I heard George call me; and looking round, I saw him standing gazing up at the roof of the cavern above his head.

"Master Eden, come here a minute, sir," he said.

I turned on my heel and obeyed, wondering what he wanted.

"Look here, sir," he continued, as I reached his side. "D'you see that hole up above there? I wonder how far it goes."

The roof of the cave was almost lost to view in sombre shadows; but as I have already mentioned, our eyes had become sufficiently accustomed to the gloom to make out the existence of a curious hole or fissure in the rock, which resembled nothing so much as a wide old-fashioned chimney, and this resemblance was strengthened by the fact that one side of it was level with the end wall of the cavern. More than this we could not tell, an oblong patch of blackness being all that could be seen from where we stood.

"I believe it goes up some way," continued George. "I noticed that the smoke from the fire all went up it, and didn't hang about in the roof yonder; and last night I heard the wind rushing through the opening when the big waves burst into the cavern."

"There are plenty of funny holes worn in the rook along this coast," I replied. "It may go up for a few feet, but there's no chance of its leading out to the top of the cliff."

"No, I don't suppose it would," answered my companion; "but what I've been thinking is, that perhaps it may turn a bit, and so form a ledge where we might take refuge out of reach of the waves."

"But it's out of our reach," I answered, almost petulantly. "We can't climb up the side of a flat rock like flies up a window-pane."

George did not reply for a moment, but remained staring upwards with his head thrown back as far as it would go.

"I believe," he continued, "that if we climbed up to the ledge we were on last night, and I hoisted you on to my shoulders, you might get a foothold still higher up on that shelf. Then there's a crack just below the opening, and if you stuck that piece of plank that's left in the rift, it would make another step, and bring you practically right into the hole. I suppose you've never climbed a chimney, Master Eden; but if you could do as the climbing boys do, work yourself up with your back against one side and your knees against the other, you might see how far it goes. I'll stand below and catch you if you fall."

By the "Foxes" I was accounted one of the best climbers of the tribe, and had a steady head; but I own I was not taken with the guard's proposal. The jagged rock on which we stood was hard and cruel, and it seemed impossible to ascend and descend the shaft without a tumble.

"How about yourself?" I objected. "If I do find a ledge up there, you'll have to stay down below; we can't both stand on each other's shoulders at the same time, and that's necessary for making the start."

"There's that rope, sir," was the reply. "You might find a way of making one end fast; and if so, I'd soon be up after you."

There was a pause.

"It's our only chance, sir," said George. "There's no knowing but what it might save the two of us."

That last remark fired my resolution: it was for him as well as for myself that the attempt was to be made. He had certainly saved my life, and by all the laws of justice and honour I owed him a like return, if such a thing were possible.

"All right," I cried; "I'll try it—now, at once!"

With some difficulty we wrenched the piece of splintered plank from the cranny into which one end had been forced by the sea, after which we scrambled up the ledge on which we had passed those awful hours of darkness. Everywhere the rock was wet and slippery from the drenching it had received during the storm. I felt George's foot slide as I clambered up on to his shoulders, and a horrid feeling of faintness seized me, for I was then high enough to have broken my neck if we had fallen. With dogged determination to get as far as I could, I planted my foot on the narrow shelf which my companion had indicated; and receiving the piece of plank which he handed up, I thrust it into the crack some two feet higher up, and almost in what might be called the mouth of the chimney. Fortunately this crevice was just wide enough to admit the wood a sufficient distance to make it secure; another step upwards, and as I made it my head struck sharply against something projecting from the side of the hole. It was evidently an iron bar bent round in a semicircle, with both ends embedded firmly in the rock. The surface was eaten with rust, but pull and tug at it as I would, it showed no signs of giving. Rising carefully to my full height, I found another piece of iron exactly similar to the first some little way above; then suddenly it occurred to my mind that they had been put there to serve as steps, as I had once seen similar irons placed in a new chimney-stack at Castlefield. Hesitating no longer, I mounted from one to another, until I must have climbed a dozen; then feeling with my hand in the darkness, I discovered an open space, evidently the mouth of some subterranean tunnel.

Far beneath me I could just make out the pale shadow of my companion's upturned face as he gazed anxiously into the gloom, wondering, no doubt, what had become of me.

"George! George!" I yelled excitedly, "I've found the entrance of a passage. Come up quick, and see for yourself. I believe we're saved!"

CHAPTER XVI.

THE SUBTERRANEAN TUNNEL.

Whether George understood me I could not tell; he made some reply, but my increasing deafness rendered his words inaudible, I shouted again, and told him of the iron steps I had discovered; and this time he must have heard, for he waved his hand. He disappeared, but after a few moments I saw him again.

"Catch the end of this rope, and make it fast if you can," he roared.

Twice he threw, and I heard the coil of rope whistle in the rocky shaft, but it did not reach my hand; then the third time I grabbed it, and to make doubly sure, I fastened it to two of the iron steps, in case one should not prove equal to the strain of George's weight.

Woodley was an active fellow. He swung on the rope first, to make certain that it would bear him, and then commenced to climb. In less than two minutes he was by my side.

"Well, this is a queer place," he remarked, as he crouched by me in the subterranean tunnel. "Those iron steps weren't put there for nothing; somebody must have used them for going up and down."

"I wonder where this passage goes?" I said. "Perhaps it's part of a disused mine."

"There never was no mine along here that I know of," answered my companion. "The air seems fresh. The only thing is to go along and see where it leads. Be careful, Master Eden; there may be a nasty drop somewhere."

Slowly and cautiously, in the inky darkness, we crept along, at each step making sure of the ground in front of us before we advanced further. The path appeared to make a very gradual slope upwards. We must have gone quite twenty yards, which, owing to our slow progress, seemed treble that distance, and we were beginning to exult in the thought of speedily obtaining our freedom, when there was an exclamation from George, and the next moment we found ourselves brought up short by a bank of earth which completely blocked the passage. Even in the darkness it was not difficult to realize what had happened.

"The roof has fallen in," said Woodley shortly, but the catch in his voice betrayed his bitter disappointment.

There was no help for it—the tunnel was blocked; and in utter weariness we sat down on the rocky floor to rest.

"Well, we're better off here than where we were last night," said George. "We shouldn't live many more hours down below, for I believe the storm's getting worse."

"I wonder what this passage was for?" I remarked, after a few moments' silence. "D'you suppose the smugglers used it for anything?"

"No," answered George. "If the smugglers made it, then old Lewis would have known of its existence, and he'd have tried to escape this way instead of risking his life in that boat."

"He did say something," I exclaimed, suddenly remembering the last words I had heard from the old salt. "I didn't suppose they had any meaning at the time, for I thought he was drunk. Wait a moment, and I'll tell you exactly what they were. He said, 'You'll find it yourself if you look about. I'm the only one as knows.'"

"Then he must have known," said George, "but he didn't want those convict chaps to find out. Perhaps it's a secret among the 'free traders,' or perhaps it's a fact that the old chap was really the only person who knew. I've heard him say that he was a rare climber when he was younger, and had got to places on the cliffs where no one else had ever been. Well, sir, there's a bit of cheese and two apples wedged in that crack of the rock. I'd better go down and fetch them before the tide rises; they'll at least keep life in us for a couple of days."

Slowly we retraced our steps, taking great care lest we should arrive at the opening of the shaft before we knew where we were, and fall through it on to the platform beneath. With the sea rising, there seemed as small a chance as ever that we should get out of the cave alive; but we were, at all events, spared the terrible fate which that morning had seemed inevitable. Woodley descended to the cavern, and having rolled up the two apples and the cheese in his coat, he made fast the bundle to the end of the rope, and I hauled it up. He was in the act of following, and had nearly reached the mouth of the shaft, when I saw him pause and, hanging on the rope with one hand, take something off a ledge with the other.

"What d'you think I've found?" he said, as he joined me again in the tunnel. "Why, that pistol Rodwood left behind. I put it right up there out of harm's way. The little crevice is dry and sheltered, and a good bit above the reach of the waves, so I don't doubt but what the charge will explode all right if it's fired. It don't seem much good to us at present, but it might come in useful to make a signal and attract attention if we could manage to get to the mouth of the cave and sight a passing ship or boat. There!" he continued, as we once more sat down at the end of the passage, and he unrolled our meagre stores from his coat; "that's all we've got in the world, barring the water that trickles down the rock below, and a bottle of sweet oil I've got in my pocket, which my missis asked me to bring her from the chemist's at Welmington. Poor girl! she's wondering what's become of it, and of me, too, by now, I expect. And the stuff isn't much good to us, I fancy. I wish the bottle had been filled with some of that brandy those rascals wasted; we shall be likely to need something of the sort before long, if we haven't wanted it already."

Although the tunnel was blocked, a cold draught from the cave below seemed to be always blowing through it, every now and again coming in stronger gusts as the storm increased. The darkness was so intense that I already felt it oppressive, and thought that after a time it would become positively unbearable.

"I wonder if the smugglers ever come here now," I said. "They might perhaps know of the place, and use it as a hiding-place for their goods."

With this notion in my mind I went down on my hands and knees, and felt about in order to find anything which might prove that the tunnel had been visited at one time or another by the "free traders." But though I spent some time in groping about in this manner, I picked up nothing but a few fragments of rock. Then I remembered Lewis's words, and how he had distinctly stated that he was "the only one that knows." He had no doubt been led by some accident to discover the shaft and the passage, and had thought fit to keep the knowledge to himself, perhaps intending to make good use of it when any special need should arise for a place of concealment, either for men or "goods."

I sat down again by Woodley, and passing my hand over my clothes to find if they were drying at all, I felt something hard in my inside coat pocket. Wondering vaguely what it could be, I unbuttoned my jacket, and while doing so remembered suddenly the metal tinder-box I had found in the empty desk the day before I left school. I took it out, fumbled with my fingers till I found the flint and steel, and—I suppose for the sake of seeing a ray of light, however tiny and momentary—I struck a spark. I hardly think if I had fired a gun it could have produced a more unexpected effect on Woodley. He sprang to his feet with something like a shout of surprise.

"What's that?" he cried. "A tinder-box! Where did you find it? I made sure Rodwood had taken it with him in his pocket."

"This is another," I answered; "it's one I found at school. The lid fits well, and has kept out the damp, I fancy."

"Bless the boy!" cried George, "why didn't you tell me you had it before? I've been wishing and wishing for one this last hour or more."

"It's precious little good now that you have got it," I replied, handing him the box in the darkness. "We've got nothing to light except the tinder and matches, and that's no practical use."

"Wait a bit," interrupted the guard. "We'll make a lamp. This bottle of oil I've got in my pocket will provide stuff to burn, and a strand of worsted out of one of my socks will make a wick. Hurrah, Master Eden! we'll get a light burning presently, and find out what sort of a place we're in."

"I don't see how you're going to make a lamp," I answered, "unless you hold the oil in the palm of your hand. We've got nothing left—not even that metal cup the men took from poor Tom's flask."

The question was a difficult one to answer. Reduced to the possession of practically nothing but the clothes we wore, it seemed at first impossible to manufacture any implement or vessel, however simple. But necessity is the mother of invention, and certainly the necessity in our case was sufficiently pressing to quicken any inventive faculties we might possess.

After some minutes' thought, and the making of one or two suggestions which had to be abandoned as impracticable, my companion slapped his thigh, exclaiming,—

"I've got it—my old watch!"

With the aid of his knife George managed to remove the works from the old-fashioned turnip-shaped silver case, which was so commonly seen in those days. This formed a sort of cup to hold the oil, which was supplied with a sort of floating wick made of a thread of worsted and a tiny bit of wood, to obtain which we were obliged to descend the iron steps, and bring up the fragment of broken plank from the bottom of the shaft. It was hardly possible that the tiny flame could be kept long alight if exposed to the strong draught which swept through the tunnel; but with a piece of leather cut from the top of his boot, and the big bull's-eye glass of the watch, Woodley managed to fashion a rough but effective shade, and at length the lamp was pronounced ready for use. If we had been a couple of boys about to let off a big sky-rocket, we could hardly have felt more excited as we struck the flint, blew up the spark in the tinder, and ignited first the sulphur match and then the tiny wick. The result was poor enough, but the lamp certainly did burn, giving out perhaps as much light as a modern night-light. To us, however, after having been so long in total darkness, it seemed quite brilliant; and with its aid there was at all events a possibility of our being able to examine our surroundings.

A part of the passage had evidently been cut through the solid rock, but farther along the roof was of earth, and had been propped up with wooden supports. It was owing to the fact that some of these, no doubt rotten with age, had given way, that the fall had occurred which formed the block against which we had been brought up short. We at once proceeded to examine this obstruction, and had hardly turned our light upon it before we made an important discovery. The fall had not been of sufficient volume to quite block the tunnel; there was a narrow opening still at the top of the heap of *débris*, but not wide enough, as we could see at a glance, to admit of the passage of a human being.

"Hurrah!" cried the guard. "D'you see that, sir? We'll soon scratch a hole there big enough to crawl through, or my name ain't George Woodley."

"I'm afraid if you do it won't be much good," I answered. "If the roof has fallen here, it's almost sure to have fallen again further on in several places, before the tunnel comes to the surface. This shows that no one has been along it for some time."

We turned away, and examined the rest of the passage as far as the top of the shaft; but only one thing did we find, and that was an empty bottle stowed away in a hole in the rock. It was a queer, misshapen old thing, which had, perhaps, held good liquor in its time, but evidently belonged to a by-gone age. Worthless as it might have appeared under ordinary circumstances, to us it proved a valuable find; and George offered at once to go down and fill it with water from the cave below. The discovery and the suggestion were both made none too soon. Another half-hour and it would have been impossible, for both wind and tide were rising; the big waves were already breaking into the entrance of the cavern with a booming roar, and the boiling surf swept clean over the platform just as George was re-ascending the rope.

I was a strong, healthy boy, but the long hours of cold, terror, and semi-starvation were beginning to tell. I felt weak and feverish, my skin was dry and parched, yet the chill from my sodden clothes seemed still to strike right through into my very bones. With the aid of his knife George fashioned the fragment of plank into something resembling a short spade; then scrambling up the bank of earth, he began to dig with the intention of enlarging the existing hole till it should be big enough for us to crawl through. With burning eyes and chattering teeth I stood below, and assisted as best I could by dragging away the loose earth with my hands. What with my deafness, and with the roar of the sea in the cavern below, I could not hear a word he said, though he did not waste much time in talking.

Our fate must have been decided long before this if we had not found means of ascending the shaft to our present position. The storm had increased in fury, and we could tell each time a big wave swept into the cavern, by the rush of air which came whistling up the shaft and swept in a briny blast along the passage. Suddenly George stopped working, and I saw the dark outline of his figure motionless in the feeble ray of the little lamp.

"What's the matter?" I cried.

He made no reply, but raised his hand as a person would in the act of listening. For half a minute he remained in that position, then resumed his digging. In a very short time, however, he stopped again, and after an instant's pause startled me by leaning forward and shouting at the top of his voice through the hole,—

"Hollo, there!"

Receiving apparently no reply to his hail, he turned and beckoned me to climb up by his side.

"Can you hear anything, Master Eden?" he asked.

I listened intently, but no sound caught my ear but the muffled surge and splash of the water in the cavern.

"There!" exclaimed my companion—"there again! Don't you hear it?"

Still to my dulled hearing no fresh sound was audible.

"What was it?" I asked.

Without answering my question, he once more roared, "Hollo, there!" through the widened hole, and remained with warning hand uplifted, as though expecting an answering shout. "Fancy, I suppose," he muttered at length. "Yet that blind fellow heard something of the sort too. Tut! I think I'm going queer in my head."

He went on digging, but once or twice I noticed that he paused in the same curious manner. I was too weary to pay much attention, but continued laboriously scooping and dragging the earth he loosened till my fingers seemed raw. At length Woodley stopped digging, and sat down for a rest. As he moved the lamp the dim oil flame gave me a momentary glimpse of his face, and on it I thought I detected a queer expression which I had never noticed there before.

For ten minutes, perhaps, he sat regaining his breath, and saying nothing; then turning to me he asked abruptly,—

"Master Eden, do you believe there's such things as ghosts?"

"No," I answered blankly, astonished at the question. A terrible thought flashed through my mind that, as a last crowning horror, Woodley was actually going out of his mind. "No," I repeated in a faltering tone, "I don't believe in ghosts."

"Neither do I, then," said George; and picking up his wooden spade, he went on digging.

CHAPTER XVII.

DAYLIGHT AT LAST.

How that night passed, or whether it was night or day, I cannot say. Worn out, I must have fallen asleep over my work; and when I awoke, George was shaking my arm and informing me that he had crawled through the hole and found the passage free on the other side. I seemed to be burning hot now; there was a singing in my head, and as I rose to my feet I staggered and almost fell. How many hours George had been at work I had no idea. My notions of time were getting hazy and uncertain; I felt that we had lived in that dark, windy passage for ages.

The hole had been enlarged just sufficiently to admit of our crawling through. The fall of earth did not extend many yards, and beyond it we found ourselves in the continuation of the tunnel. On, on, on we went, moving slowly, with only the uncertain light of the tiny lamp to warn us of any dangerous pitfall which might lie in our path. Contrary to my expectation, we encountered no further obstacle of a similar kind to that through which we had just cut our way. Now we were passing once more through solid rock, and now the tunnel was continued through earth, supported by rough-hewn beams, black with damp and age. Owing to our slow progress, the distance seemed much longer than it no doubt really was; the path sloped upward with a gentle gradient all the way, and so long did the ascent appear that at almost every step I wondered that we did not arrive at the surface of the ground on a level with the top of the cliffs. The passage made no turns, and we were evidently striking straight inland. The air still kept fresh, and even at this distance from the cave we could feel the upward blast of air as the big seas entered the cavern.

I staggered along like one in a dream, sometimes steadying myself with my hands as I lurched up against rock or beam; then all at once George, who was going on a pace or two in front, started back so quickly that he trod on my toes, and nearly knocked me down. At the same moment the lamp fell from his hand, and we were once more in a darkness that could be felt.

I heard it myself that time! Out of the inky blackness, from the direction in which we were going, there came a most unearthly sound, half human, half the note of some strange instrument made and played upon by underground goblins of old country folk's tales. It rose to almost a shriek at its loudest pitch, and then died away into a sort of crooning growl. So weird and terrifying was it in that subterranean region, that, though past caring for most things, whether good or ill, I felt the hair bristle on my head.

Woodley was a brave man, as I had reason to know, but I felt his arm shaking as I clutched it with my hand.

"Hullo!—hullo, there!" he cried, in a hoarse, quavering voice which no friend of his could have recognized. "Who are you, and what are you doing?"

Once more there was no reply. Another few moments of that suspense, and I verily believe I should have turned and rushed back along the way we had come, regardless whether I ended up by pitching head first down the shaft into the cavern beneath. Fortunately, George possessed a large stock of that dogged resolution peculiar to a Briton, which desperate circumstances tend only to harden; and now, recovering from the shock which the sound had given him, I believe he was ready to deal with a whole churchyardful of ghosts.

"Strike a light, Master Eden," he said shortly, "and I'll find the lamp."

Owing partly to the fright, and partly to my dazed condition, I struck a good many blows with the steel before I had a spark glowing in the tinder. In the meantime Woodley had recovered the lamp, and replenished the oil which had been spilt by pouring out a fresh supply from the bottle in his pocket. Just as we got the wick to burn, another weird, high-pitched howl rang through the darkness, continued for perhaps half a minute, and then ceased; but this time George remained undaunted.

"You carry the lamp, sir," he said. "Hold it well up, and I'll go in front."

He took something from his pocket, and I knew from the sharp click that he had cocked the pistol.

What we expected to see it would be hard to say. Certainly not the obstacle which, a few paces further on, we found blocking our path. This was nothing more or less than a heavy wooden door, dark with age like the beams of the tunnel, and studded with rusty iron nails. We stopped, and stood staring at it in the faint glimmer of our feeble lamp. What, then, could have become of the creature—goblin or human—that had terrified us with its unearthly music? Could it have retreated before our advance, and be now lying in wait for us behind that mass of ancient timber?

Woodley was the first to move. He walked up to the door, tried it with his shoulder, and finding it fast, rapped on it with his knuckles, as though he expected some ghostly porter to answer his summons.

Again we stood, waiting and listening; then, just as I was about to speak, a gust of air came sweeping down the passage, causing our lamp to flicker, and the ghostly music burst out again close to where we stood, as though the goblin minstrel were piping defiance at us from the farther side of the door. I grabbed Woodley by the arm; but to my surprise the man burst into a roar of laughter, which mingled strangely with the weird howl that rose and fell in total disregard of this audacious interruption.

"Ho, ho!" laughed George. "To think that we should have been scared by that! Bless me, nothing but the wind blowing through a keyhole!"

A moment's examination proved his statement to be correct. The gusts of air driven along the tunnel transformed the wide, old-fashioned keyhole into a sort of musical instrument; something in the formation of the lock must, I think, have lent itself to producing an unusually strange effect as the wind hummed and whistled through the hole. Here, at all events, was an explanation to the mystery; but in my case the sudden relaxing of overstrung nerves made me little inclined to join in my companion's laugh. I leaned up against the side of the passage, gasping for breath, while the throbbing of my heart seemed to hammer through my whole frame.

By the time I had somewhat recovered from the reaction caused by our discovery, George had carefully examined the door. It was fast and firm as a rock, though on one side, where the ponderous framework seemed to have shrunk or sunk, there were chinks into which I could have inserted the end of my finger; through these, too, the stronger gusts of air sighed and hummed as though in accompaniment to the whoop and wail of the keyhole.

"It's the lock that holds it," said George, returning to my hands the lamp which he had borrowed to aid him in his investigations. "If we could find one of these beams or uprights loose, and use it as a battering-ram, we might soon burst it open."

What the object of a door in such a place could be we had no notion, nor, I believe, did we trouble to think. What concerned us was that it stood between us and our hopes of liberty; and having no tool with which to pick the lock, we must employ our remaining strength in an attempt to make it yield to force.

To this end we retraced our steps some distance along the passage; but the heavy blocks of timber were too firmly fixed to admit of our wrenching them from their places. In vain did we search for a lump of rock sufficiently large and heavy to answer the same purpose; the only loose piece we could find was about the size of a man's boot, and we might have continued to fling this at the door for a whole week without achieving any further result than dinting the oak.

"Master Eden," said George, turning to me as though a sudden thought had come into his mind, "I've got a key here I fancy will fit that lock," and he made a sign indicating the pistol in his hand. "I've heard of its being done," he continued, "and I don't see why it shouldn't act in this case. I'll extract the ball, put the end of the muzzle to the keyhole, and blow the lock clean off the inside of the door. The powder's dry, and I don't doubt but what it'll explode."

"You'll hurt your hand," I said.

"I'll chance that," he replied. "I'll use my left. Now, sir, you hold the lamp, and stand clear when I fire."

With the corkscrew belonging to his knife Woodley was able to draw the wad from the short-barrelled pistol, and so remove the ball; then standing at arm's-length from the door, he took the weapon in his left hand and signalled to me to go farther back. The next instant there was a blinding flash, and a report which, in that confined space, sounded like the discharge of a small cannon. Woodley staggered back, and his arm dropped to his side. It was not for some moments that I was able to ascertain whether or not he was seriously injured; then it turned out that the recoil of the firearm, discharged with its muzzle so close to the door, had dislocated his wrist.

We pressed forward through the cloud of pungent smoke, and to our delight found that the door was no longer able to resist our united efforts to shove it open; indeed, when we had time to examine it more closely, we found that the lock had been blown away on the inside. We crossed the threshold eagerly enough, but the next moment whatever hopes had risen in our minds of finding ourselves on the point of stepping out into the blessed fresh air and light of day were dashed to the ground. We had certainly arrived at the end of our journey, but only to find that the long tunnel had apparently no outlet, and terminated in a small underground cell, of which the walls and roof even were of stone. As the dim light of our lamp revealed this unwelcome truth, I felt that at last our fate was finally sealed, that I could make no further effort, and that here I must lie down and die. Listlessly I stood by George's side and looked round. The little chamber in which we stood was the same height as the tunnel, and, I should say, as regards length and breadth not more than five feet square. It contained nothing but a three-legged wooden stool, and an ancient box or coffer, apparently of iron, secured with a heavy padlock. The walls, as I have said, were of roughly-hewn stone, and the roof was formed of two slabs of granite. Dimly I wondered to what purpose such a place could ever have been put—whether some hermit had dwelt there in a bygone age, and why such a long tunnel had been excavated for no further purpose than to end in a tiny vault which seemingly, to all intents and purposes, might have been constructed immediately above the cave. These thoughts drifted languidly through my fevered brain; the reaction after a brief period of excitement was beginning to tell, and I was fast coming to the end of my powers of endurance.

"What's this, I wonder?" exclaimed George, giving the iron box a kick. "Some old pirate's treasure, maybe. Well, if 'twas full of gold it's no good to us at present, nor likely to be unless we can find a way out of this vault. Set down the light a moment, Master Eden," he continued. "I'll hoist you up on my back, sir, and you can see if you can stir either of them stone slabs overhead."

Feeble as I was, I doubt whether I could have moved the stone if it had offered no other resistance than its own weight; as it was, for all the effect my pushing had there might have been ten thousand tons of earth resting on its upper surface. As Woodley once more set me on my feet I turned giddy, and sank down on the iron box to save myself from falling. The dimly-lit vault spun round and round; I leaned my head against the cold stone and closed my eyes.

Whether I fainted or merely dozed off from sheer exhaustion I can't say, but after what seemed an age I was roused by Woodley shaking my shoulder and addressing me in loud and excited tones. His words had to be repeated several times before I grasped their meaning; then at last they forced themselves into my brain.

"Master Eden, I've heard a dog barking! There 'tis again! Liven up, sir; we can't be far from help."

For a moment I seemed to recover full possession of my senses; my brain was feverishly active as a sudden inspiration came to my mind—the weird song of the wind through the keyhole, the long uphill slope of the passage, the barking of the dog.

"George," I cried, "I know where we are! We're in the secret place at Coverthorne! We must be close to the haunted room, perhaps directly under it; and the wind was the ghost!" I broke out into a fit of wild hysterical laughter, and ended by bursting into tears.

"Steady, steady, sir," cried George. "What d'you mean? What are you talking about?"

With an effort recovering my self-possession, I told him in a few words what I meant, and how I believed we had unwittingly discovered the old house's secret chamber.

"But what can we do?" I exclaimed. "We may stay buried here for any length of time, and no one know where we are or how to get us out."

Woodley was certainly a man of quick resource. He stood thinking for a moment; then picking up the lamp, he carried it out into the tunnel, and returning closed the door. Standing in the pitch darkness, we saw for the first time a faint gray shadow as it were, but a few inches long, which filtered through between one granite slab and the end wall of the cell. Faint and indistinct it might be, but at the sight of it our hearts leaped within us: this was daylight at last!

"Hurrah!" shouted George. "Yonder's the way out? Now I'll soon have some one to open the door for us, or may I never ride behind four horses again!"

He brought back the lamp, and then commenced to yell at the top of his voice, varying this proceeding by hurling the wooden stool up against the slabs overhead, which, in spite of the injury to his left arm, he continued doing till every leg was smashed and only the seat remained.

"Yo-ho!" he shouted. "The dog's heard me; he's barking like mad. Yo-ho! help here—help!"

I made some feeble attempt to contribute to the uproar, but my voice seemed suddenly to have failed me, and my cheer was nothing but a croak. Strange noises were ringing in my ears, and a shower of sparks danced before my eyes.

How long this continued I could not have told, but at length there was a muffled, "Who are you down there?" and more shouting on the part of George. Then I became aware of the fact that Woodley was hugging me in his arms, laughing and crying, and assuring me that we were saved.

Straightway I found myself mounted with him on the back seat of a coach. We were tearing along at breakneck speed in the twilight of a winter afternoon; there was a great roaring in the air, which drowned even the rattle of the wheels, and looking round I was horrified to see following us a great onrushing wall of water, as though the sea had overflowed the land. Faster and faster became our wild gallop, but the huge line of breakers was gaining on us every moment; now we were overtaken, and a great wave was rearing its head above us to sweep us to destruction. I heard a muffled voice shout, "Stand from under!" There was a crash, a blaze of light, and I became unconscious.

Long after, whole centuries later it might have been, I became aware of the fact that I was staring upward at some oblong patch of light. Slowly this resolved itself into an opening in the roof of the passage, and I realized that two men and a boy were staring down at me in mute astonishment. Then, as my dizzy brain grew clear for a moment, I recognized the last named as Miles Coverthorne.

Once more the roar of a troubled sea was in my ears; I had a horrible idea that I had been thrust down into a vault and should be buried alive. I made one last frantic effort to retain my failing senses.

"Miles," I cried pitifully, "take me out! Don't let them bury me! I'm Sylvester Eden!"

I could not hear his reply, but saw him move his head and hand, and the next moment I had been whirled away once more into darkness beyond even the land of dreams.

CHAPTER XVIII.

A FURTHER FIND.

I awoke quite naturally, as though from a deep sleep, to find myself in bed, with Mrs. Coverthorne and a strange gentleman standing close by, looking down at me as I lay. I recognized the room, and had some hazy idea that this was a continuation of my summer holiday.

"Well?" said the gentleman, smiling; "feeling better after your nap?"

I felt too drowsy to reply, but languidly allowed the stranger to feel my pulse, which he did after lugging a huge watch out of his fob.

"Keep him snug in bed for a day or two," I heard him say, "and he'll be all right. Forty years ago I dare say I could have gone through it myself without much hurt. I'll make up something, and send it by the boy."

I was asleep again before they left the room, and did not wake till Mrs. Coverthorne roused me to take some beef tea. Slowly, as I swallowed the nourishment, I began to wonder why I was propped up in bed, being fed with a spoon in my old room at Coverthorne. Had I been ill? or had I met with an accident? What had Miles and I been doing? Then suddenly, like a landscape coming into view through a quickly-vanishing mist, the recollection of past events came flooding into my mind. I remembered it all now—the captured coach, the sea cavern, and the dark subterranean tunnel.

"George!" I cried—"George Woodley! Is he safe? He was with me in the passage."

"Yes, he's quite safe," answered Mrs. Coverthorne, with a smile. "He's down in the kitchen now, having his dinner. You shall see him again by-and-by, but just for the present you must keep very quiet and not talk."

172

It seemed no hardship for the time being to lie warm and snug in bed, and in the wakeful intervals between my dozes I recalled and pieced together the whole story of our adventure. Once when I woke I was surprised to find Mr. Denny in the room, standing gazing out of the window with his hands under his coat tails. Some slight movement on my part caused him to turn; he smiled and nodded, and moved towards the bed.

"Feeling as if you could relish a good beef-steak and slice of pudding?" he inquired.

"Not just yet," I answered feebly. "O Mr. Denny," I continued, remembering something which, since my return of memory, had been puzzling my brain, "was that the secret place that George and I discovered?"

"Yes," he answered; "but I fancy you discovered something more important than the hidden chamber." He said this with a dry chuckle, and producing his little tortoise-shell box took a pinch of snuff.

"What was that?" I asked languidly.

"Well, I don't think you'd understand if I told you. Better wait, and you shall hear all in good time."

I must have slept most of that day. Thanks to my youth and good constitution, I was suffering from nothing worse than exhaustion and a severe cold, and I was much stronger when Miles came to see me the following morning.

He had already heard our story from George Woodley; indeed, I think that by this time there was hardly a man, woman, or child on the whole countryside but had listened to a more or less exaggerated narrative of our adventures. In some of these garbled accounts George and I were reported to have done and endured the most extraordinary things. One old lady, to her dying day, could never be persuaded otherwise than that the convicts had locked us inside the coach, and then sent us and it together bodily over the cliff.

"I shall never forget when we first heard that strange muffled knocking and shouting in the west parlour," said

Miles. "It was so strange and unearthly that my blood ran cold with terror. John, the shepherd, was in the yard, and noticed that his dog seemed uneasy, and kept barking and growling at something. I was talking with him at the time. We paused to listen, but I could hear nothing; so John ordered the dog to lie down. Old 'Help' still kept grumbling to himself; then, just as the man and I were turning to walk out of the yard, one of the maids came out of the house screaming and bawling something about a ghost. It was some seconds before we could get enough sense out of her to understand what was wrong, and in the meantime Stokes, the wagoner, came clattering out of the stable and joined the group. There was a ghost knocking and calling in the haunted room, so the girl informed us, and off we went to discover what was wrong. Old John shortened his oak stick, and Stokes caught up a pitchfork: they evidently both meant business.

"It seems funny enough now, but I can tell you I didn't feel much inclined to laugh when we reached that fusty old parlour and heard that mysterious bump, bump, and a faint, far-off voice, as it seemed, giving unearthly whoops, and crying, 'Help!' Old John was the first to recover his senses. 'There's some one under here!' he cried, striking his stick on the hearthstone. Then he shouted, and sure enough there was an answering hail. It seemed impossible that any living being could be down under that solid slab of granite; but we fetched a pick and crowbar, and worked at it till it fell into the tunnel. If we'd only known the proper way to deal with it, we could have made it slide along into a recess specially made for it at the back of the fireplace, but we didn't discover that till later.

"Woodley says you fainted; but fortunately he heard our warning shout to stand from under, and dragged you back into the tunnel, or you might have been killed by the falling slab. I was so excited and astonished as I looked down into that queer little vault, and you both were so haggard, and ragged, and generally bedraggled, that at first I didn't recognize you, and it was only when you called my name that I saw who it was. Well, you may be very sure we soon had you out; and I think you know the rest."

"The room will never be haunted any more," I said, laughing; "George laid the ghost with his pistol. But tell me, when did you first know that the convicts had escaped?"

"We heard about the coach having been seized the very next morning. The alarm of their escape was given very much sooner than the men expected. It so happened that a labourer had come into Rockymouth to fetch the doctor for his child, who was very ill. Dr. Thomas—who came to see you yesterday—was out in the country, and the man hurried off to catch him before he returned home. Going along the road in the darkness, he heard the trampling of horses' hoofs, and the sound of a heavy vehicle coming towards him, and so stepped aside into a gateway. None of your gang saw him; but, as you can imagine, he was mightily surprised to see a mail-coach and team come jolting and floundering down that byroad. Fortunately for him he didn't hail it; but he thought something must be wrong, and he spoke about it when he met the doctor. As luck would have it, Dr. Thomas, on his return journey, had to go some distance along the highroad, and there he was accosted by a man who was out of breath with running. This fellow turned out to be one of the warders; he had managed to get the gag out of his mouth and shout for help till some one came and untied his bonds. His story was soon told, and Dr. Thomas rode as fast as he could back to Rockymouth, and gave the alarm. George says you heard him coming just before you got into the boat.

"For a time the whole place was in a state of panic, and every person who lived in outlying cottages was expecting to be robbed, and perhaps murdered, by the convicts. A large body of men, armed with all kinds of weapons, from a gun to a reaping-hook, went out to hunt for them, but with no result. Then a boat was seen floating bottom upwards some distance from shore, and the report got about that the gang had attempted to cross to France, but being landsmen had overturned the boat, and were all drowned.

"The question which puzzled most people was what had become of the *True Blue*, and the general opinion was that one or more of the men had not gone with the others, but had stuck to the coach, and driven it somewhere right away on to the moors. It was only yesterday that the horses were found and identified."

"Were all the convicts drowned?" I asked.

"Very little doubt, I fear," was the reply. "There's a reef of rocks just outside the mouth of that cave which, when the sea is at all rough, makes a strong current and dangerous eddy. It's almost certain that as soon as the boat got clear of the mouth of the cavern she was caught in the swirl and swung round, and the men jumping up, or throwing themselves about in a panic, turned her over."

Miles stood for a moment silently eyeing me with a curious look on his face.

"I say, Sylvester," he began again, lowering his voice, "promise me you won't say anything, but I believe one of them was saved."

"Who—old Lewis?" I asked excitedly.

My companion nodded.

"I've just heard the faintest rumour that his dog dragged him ashore on a ledge below what's called the Old Quarry. At all events, the dog's on land, and I take care not to ask too many questions about Lewis. A man brought me a curious message, telling me to 'go down to the seal-cave by the short cut, and see what I should find.' I couldn't make head or tail out of it, and the man didn't seem to know the sense of it either, but said it had been given him to pass on by a friend. Now, when I come to think it over, I believe Lewis must sometime have discovered the tunnel and hiding-place. He imagined I should know of them too, and he thought he ought not to give the secret away to other people. I suppose he judged this hint would be sufficient, and that I should go down to the tunnel and rescue you and George.—By the way," added the speaker, turning on his heel to leave the room, "we've sent word to your father and mother to say you're safe, and that you'll be sent home to them as soon as you're well enough to travel."

After each long sleep I seemed to wake up stronger, and my thoughts turned to Miles and his mother, from whom I was receiving so much kindness. I remembered what the former had told me—of how his uncle meant to claim half the estate at the commencement of the New Year, which was now close at hand; and how, with straitened means, they feared it would be impossible for them to live on at Coverthorne. Several times I had been on the point of questioning Miles on the matter, but it seemed such a painful subject that the words had died on my lips.

Strangely enough, I could not but think that both he and his mother looked more cheerful than when I had visited them last; and though there still appeared an anxious expression in Mrs. Coverthorne's face, there seemed also to be an air of hope and confidence about her at which I greatly wondered.

Once there was a knock at the door, and George Woodley came to wish me good-bye. He seemed in high spirits, and to have quite recovered from the effects of our adventure, except that his left arm hung in a sling.

"My eye, Master Eden!" he exclaimed, "for the same rate of pay I believe I'd go through it all again!"

"What d'you mean?" I asked.

"Why, look here, sir," he continued, producing a crisp five-pound note from his pocket. "That there Mr. Denny gave me this! I didn't want to take it, but he said I deserved it for laying the ghost. What's more, I'm thinking before long of giving up the road and settling down in a little dairy-farm business, which the missis and I could look after between our two selves; and Master Miles has promised, when I do, that he'll start my stock with one of the best beasts he's got on the farm. Well, good-bye, sir. I hope I shall see you again quite well when you're on your way back to school in January."

Liberal I knew the Coverthornes always were, but it astonished me rather that they should bestow such handsome gifts on Woodley, to whom they were really under no obligation. If it had been my own parents, the case would have been different; for the man had certainly saved my life, and I fully intended to ask my father to send him a suitable reward.

On the third day after my strange and unceremonious arrival at the old house, I was so far recovered as to be able to get up in the afternoon and spend a few hours downstairs. Being for a time alone with Miles in the parlour, my thoughts returned to the subject of his future.

"Miles," I said, "do tell me what you are going to do next year. Is your uncle Nicholas still determined to take away half the land?"

"As far as I know, that's his intention—at present," was the reply.

There was something about the way in which the last two words were uttered which made me prick up my ears.

"Look here! why did Mr. Denny give such a handsome present to George Woodley?" I asked. "And why did you promise him that cow?"

"I suppose we can give him what presents we like, as long as the things are ours to give," retorted Miles, smiling.

Another recollection had just flashed across my mind.

"Miles, Mr. Denny said that we had discovered something more important than the hidden chamber. What did he mean?"

My companion turned away from me with a queer laugh.

"I'm under promise not to tell," he answered. "You may hear to-morrow."

CHAPTER XIX.

BROUGHT TO BAY.

It was the last day of the old year, and though burning with curiosity to know what discovery George and I had unwittingly made beyond the whereabouts of the secret chamber, I forbore to ask any questions. Remembering that after this date Miles and his mother could no longer count on being left in undisputed possession of the whole estate, I did not like to make any inquiries which might revive this painful subject; so, with an effort, I resolved to possess my soul in patience, and wait till either Miles or Mr. Denny should volunteer some explanation.

The latter had arrived at the house not long after breakfast, and appeared to have come to spend the day. From some remarks which he made, I understood that he had been in Welmington the day before, and had travelled home through the night. Considering that he was an elderly man, and that this was the middle of winter, it struck me that whatever business he had had to transact must have been both important and urgent. In some indefinable manner the impression grew in my mind that something was brewing—whether trouble or otherwise I could not say; but there was a subdued air of excitement about the house, in which Miles, his mother, and the lawyer all seemed to share. Though I cannot but own that it aroused my curiosity, I stuck to my former determination to mind my own business, and not try to poke my nose into matters in which I had no concern.

At dinner even Mr. Denny, usually so sharp and alert, seemed at times a trifle preoccupied; while Mrs. Coverthorne was evidently in a state of nervous tension. She made a forced attempt to keep up the conversation, but it was plain that she was merely talking for the sake of talking, and that her thoughts were far from the subject of her remarks. Still, whatever might have been weighing on her mind, her look seemed to denote a change from when I had seen her in the summer: it was as though some burden of care had been recently lifted from her shoulders.

When the table had been cleared, we still sat on in the oak-panelled parlour—Mr. Denny thoughtfully sipping his wine, Miles notching a small fragment of firewood with his pocket-knife, and his mother making a pretence to sew, though at times I saw her hand shake so that she could not possibly direct her needle. As no one else made a move, I, too, remained in the room, gazing at the burning logs in the big open hearth.

At length there came a sound of horses' hoofs in the yard, and I saw Mrs. Coverthorne and Mr. Denny exchange a quick glance; then, a few minutes later, one of the maids knocked at the door and announced Mr. Nicholas Coverthorne.

Miles's mother rose to her feet, letting her work drop unheeded to the floor.

"Come, Sylvester," she said; "Mr. Denny has some private business to transact, and we will go into another room."

In the passage we met Mr. Coverthorne. He paused as though about to speak, but his sister-in-law passed him with a slight inclination of her head. I saw the man's face in the half-light of the passage—grim, cold, forbidding; and so the recollection of it has always remained in my mind. He passed on with a measured stride, entered the parlour, and closed the door behind him.

It was not until some years later that I heard from the lips of my friend an exact account of the interview which followed; but so vividly was every detail of it impressed on Miles's mind that in after life he could recall it as though it had been an event of yesterday.

Mr. Denny and the visitor exchanged a formal salutation, and the latter took a chair by the side of the table. A man of iron will and unrelenting purpose, tall and heavily built, the little dried-up lawyer seemed no match for such an adversary; but he was evidently prepared for the fray, and began by politely pushing the decanter and a glass towards his opponent. Mr. Nicholas, however, declined the proffered refreshment with a somewhat peremptory wave of his hand.

"Your time, Mr. Coverthorne, I know is valuable," began the lawyer, "and therefore I know you will thank me to come at once to business. I requested you to meet me here to ask you once more whether you were finally determined to assert your claim to half the Coverthorne estate—a claim based, of course, on the will made early in the present year, under very extraordinary circumstances, by your brother James?"

An angry glint came into the visitor's cold gray eyes, but he was too strong a man to give way to any outburst of passion.

"I thought we had come to a clear and definite understanding on that point long ago," he replied. "If that is all you have to say, you have brought me here for nothing. Moreover, I strongly resent your suggestion that the will was made under any 'extraordinary circumstances.' For reasons of his own, my late brother chose to keep the matter for the time being from the knowledge of his family; but the will was executed in a perfectly proper and legal manner, as you yourself must know, having seen the document with your own eyes."

"This division of the property would necessitate your sister-in-law and her son leaving Coverthorne," said Mr. Denny.

"I don't necessarily admit that," returned the other. "But as I've told you before, sir, other people have rights to be considered besides my brother's family. He himself saw that

I had been done out of mine for many years; and though neither he nor I then thought that I should ever benefit by this act of restitution, yet he considered it just and necessary, if for nothing more than as an acknowledgment that I had not been fairly dealt with, and that I had his sympathy. I have already suggested to Mrs. Coverthorne that, as this house is much too large for her and Miles, she should give it up and take a smaller one in town, where they would see more people and make new friends."

"Still," said Mr. Denny, "it is very hard for the lad, as his father's heir, to have to give up the old house, which has been in the family for so many generations, containing, as it does, the rooms in which his great-grandparents lived and died—ay, further back still. I repeat, it would be hard for him to give up a home so rich in old traditions and associations."

"Merely a matter of sentiment," answered Mr. Nicholas shortly. "If the old place were mine, I'd sell it to-morrow if I were offered a good enough price."

"There's that secret place about which so many legends have clustered," went on the solicitor musingly, "and which you once gave us to understand was simply a hole in the chimney which had been built up in your father's time. I suppose you heard how it was discovered?"

The visitor nodded.

Mr. Denny took another sip at his port, set down the glass, and sat up straighter in his chair. There was something in his action suggestive of a person who suddenly prepares to attack after having stood for some time merely on the defensive.

"On the same day that the secret chamber was found," he began, "we made another discovery, to which I should now like to call your attention. In the underground chamber was an iron box, which on being opened was found to contain a quantity of papers. Among them was your brother's will, which since his death we had not been able to discover. He went away from home some little time ago at rather short notice, and probably deposited the documents in the hiding-place for safe-keeping."

"You mean the will which he made some three years ago?" said Mr. Nicholas.

"Exactly," answered Mr. Denny. In his quick, jerky movements he was always very like a bird, but now he was watching the other man with the keen eyes of a hawk.

"Well?" queried the visitor.

"On examination," continued the lawyer, "I found that, unknown to me, he had added a codicil. Pardon me if I make this quite clear for the benefit of our young friend," he continued, turning to Miles. "A codicil is an addition—postscript, as it were—which a person adds to his original will, and it has to be duly signed and witnessed in the same way as the will itself. In this case your father wished a small sum of money to be given to an old servant, and to ensure this being done he added the codicil of which I am speaking."

Mr. Nicholas was listening intently, but did not seem to understand at what the lawyer was driving.

"Well, what of that?" he demanded.

"The point is," said Mr. Denny quite calmly, "that this codicil was dated not more than a month before your brother's death."

A deep hush fell upon the room—so deep that the ticking of the old clock in the corner seemed to have become almost as loud as the knocking of a hammer. Mr. Nicholas sat like a graven image, merely drumming softly on the table with the tips of his fingers, while his and Mr. Denny's gaze remained fixed as though each had determined to stare the other out of countenance.

"Once more, for the benefit of our young friend, let me be more explicit," went on Mr. Denny. "His father makes a will, and then, apparently, revokes it by making another some eighteen months later. Now, a month before his death, instead of adding a codicil to the second will, he adds it to the first, which has become so much waste paper—a foolish thing, which no man in his senses would have thought of doing. We can only conclude," continued Mr. Denny, "that he had no recollection at all of having executed a second will."

The square jaw was rigid, and a dark flush overspread the visitor's temples.

"It was a mistake," he said thickly. "A slip of memory might cause any one to do a similar thing."

"Following up our first discovery," continued Mr. Denny, apparently paying no attention to this reply, "I was led to go a little further, and make a second. Remembering an account which the boys gave me of a chance meeting which they had with your old servant Tom Lance, I found him out, and had an interview with him at the barracks at Welmington. He seems a sharp fellow, and it appears had taught himself to read and write, and to read handwriting."

"Well, what about him?" asked Mr. Nicholas, in a tone of repressed anger.

"Although he would not confess it before, not even to our young friends, it appears that on the evening when you first found him alone in your parlour he was so far overcome by curiosity as to open your brass-bound box and look inside. There he found a sheet of foolscap covered with signatures, chiefly those of Mr. James Coverthorne, but also of the two other men whom we know now as the witnesses to this second will."

Mr. Nicholas muttered an oath, and brought down his fist heavily on the table. His eyes flashed, and the veins in his forehead swelled with pent-up emotion.

"Go on," he said at length; "come to the point, and let us know what you mean."

"What I mean, Mr. Coverthorne, is this," replied the other, in firm, icy tones: "for the sake of her dead husband and the son who may hand on the family name, Mrs. Coverthorne has asked me to give you this information, which I might otherwise have withheld until I had sent the law to knock at your door. To-morrow I shall commence to act on behalf of my clients. I am already in communication with your solicitor, who has this second will in his possession, and I think you will gain nothing by paying him a visit; in fact, you might be wasting valuable time by such a journey. You follow me, Mr. Coverthorne, I hope?—valuable time, sir, was what I said. Now, I think there is no reason for us to prolong this interview any further."

Muttering something below his breath, Mr. Nicholas Coverthorne rose from his chair and strode from the room. A few moments later he spurred out of the yard and galloped down the road. We heard the sound of his horse-hoofs die away in the distance; and so he passed for ever out of the knowledge of those whom he had sought to wrong.

"What did it all really mean?" was the question I put to Miles when he told me this story; for on that eventful afternoon I had only a very vague notion of what had happened.

"What did it all mean?" was the reply; "why, simply this, that my uncle was a forger. Probably he had never been guilty of such a crime before, but the fact remains that he forged that will from beginning to end, and did it so well that even Mr. Denny could detect no flaw, either in the text or in the signatures. He must have possessed more skill as a penman than any one imagined. At first we thought some expert criminal must have helped him, but the fact of Tom Lance discovering that sheet of paper covered with signatures in his desk seems to prove that he did it himself. For the sake of the family my mother did not wish him to be arrested, so gave him the opportunity to escape—a chance of which he had the good sense to avail himself, for he went off that night, and we never saw or heard anything of him again. It turned out that he was deep in debt. The house and land at Stonebank were heavily mortgaged, and as soon as it was known that he was gone, everything was seized by the creditors. He was a thoroughly bad man, and if it hadn't been for your adventure, Sylvester, he'd have turned my mother and myself out of doors before he'd done with us. Yes," insisted my old friend, seeing me about to interrupt, "we shall always consider we owe it to you and George Woodley that we are still living on in the old house. If you hadn't caused me to find the secret place, Mr. Denny would never have seen that codicil to my father's will which made him feel certain that the other was a forgery. It was that discovery, coupled with what I had already told him, that induced him to go and hunt up Tom Lance; and the two things together were enough to prove my uncle's guilt. Well, 'it's an ill wind that blows nobody good,' runs the old saying, and certainly we have cause to be thankful for the outcome of your eventful journey with the coach-load of convicts."

* * * * * * * * * *

Though the "secret place" has long ago been bricked up, the old house at Coverthorne remains much the same as it appeared when I first saw it; but a fresh generation of boys and girls have sprung up to enliven it with their laughter and frolics, and to this merry audience, around the self-same hearth from under which I was drawn up half dead that winter morning, I have told repeatedly the story of that strange adventure.

George Woodley lived to a hale and peaceful old age. He did well at his farming, and was content to hear from a distance the familiar toot of the horn on which he himself had performed for so many years. He was the same bright, good-hearted fellow to the end of his days, but he could never quite forgive the convicts for having thrown the old *True Blue* over the cliff.

"The cold-blooded villains!" he would exclaim. "If they'd left her in a field or shoved her into that dry pit, I wouldn't have minded; but to smash her on the rocks—'twas as bad as murder! Well, there! they met their punishment; and for my part I know I came out of it with a very handsome reward from Master Miles, and what's more, a good yarn to tell the boys."

THE END.